Jennifer Arthur

— and —

All the Gone

Book Two of the
Chrystellean Trilogy

Alice Salerno

Illustrations by
Kevin Langstaff and Alice Salerno

abbott press®

A DIVISION OF WRITER'S DIGEST

Abbott Press books may be ordered through booksellers or by contacting:

Abbott Press
1663 Liberty Drive
Bloomington, IN 47403
www.abbottpress.com
Phone: 1-866-697-5310

ISBN: 978-1-4582-1670-0 (sc)
ISBN: 978-1-4582-1672-4 (hc)
ISBN: 978-1-4582-1671-7 (e)

Library of Congress Control Number: 2014910404

Printed in the United States of America.

Abbott Press rev. date: 10/24/2014

To my
Newest life blessings,
Hannah, Chas, Graham, Renee,
Reilly, Kaylee,
Jonah, Laura Elizabeth
And Destry

Acknowledgments

Once again, my ongoing thanks to members of the
Valley Writers, particularly to Linda McCarty, my
dedicated aide and writing adviser, my chauffeur to
all sorts of wonderful writing places and events,
a fine author in her own right, and the sister I never had.
To Marianne Tong, who was my
rescue when my computer baffled me, and
deepest appreciation and love to Ellen McKinsey, my
lifetime friend, fellow writer, confidante, adviser, and
supporter in all phases of my life.
Plus, in memory, to Xochitl Marin, who assured me, only
hours before she stepped from this life to the next,
that I have a "gift" and I must use it.
I'm grateful to have known her.

Contents

Chapter 1

◆

Earthquake?

This story should probably start with the note. There were signs even before that, though, if Jennifer had only recognized what they meant.

For instance, there was the crack in the garage wall with the corner of a piece of pearly paper sticking out of it. Pearly paper! That ought to have told her something right there. And there was the way her marmalade-colored cat, Atta Girl, had been acting. She'd been jumpy and restless for at least a week. She acted as if she were trying to talk to Jenny again, although of course she couldn't. Not in California, anyway.

As Jenny worked at her bedroom desk, Atta Girl slept at her feet in a patch of sunlight. Jenny was trying to get her act together on a special science assignment. All she'd written so far was her name, Jennifer Arthur, Science 1A, and the date, November 6.

Jenny's mom and dad were laughing in their bedroom about something her dad had said. They were getting ready to go to early dinner at Uncle Pete and Aunt Georgia's house. Uncle Pete wasn't really Jennifer's uncle, but he was Dad's favorite cousin, and Aunt Georgia was his wife. They were a fun couple, and Dad and Mom were always in good moods when they were headed there. Jenny's younger brother, Warren, would be going too, but Jenny had to beg off so she could get her homework done—just like the lesson in front of her.

It was all about space and dimensions … depth, height, width, length, and time. Well, most of that stuff seemed pretty obvious, except for the part that said time isn't even real, that it's just some markers we make up to keep track of our lives.

Well, Jenny knew how strange time could be after the adventures she, Willa, and Atta Girl had shared in the White World. It was hard for her to believe now, but it had only been last spring when Jenny, her best friend, Willa Walker, and Atta were dragged from Jenny's backyard by a white hole in space. It eventually dropped them off on a planet where *everything* was white, even Jenny's own red hair and freckles. Then after all kinds of horrendous events, and lots of nice ones too, they found their way back home through the white hole again. And when they did get home, they found it not only wasn't any later than when they'd left; it was actually a minute or two earlier.

But Willa and her parents had moved to Southern California in August, and Jenny missed her *humongously*. Most of all she missed the great talks they used to have, especially when they were remembering their White World friends—Morgan, Nitty Gritty, Ildirmyrth, Lakeesha, and Behrrn—plus all their other friends on the White World. There was no one around to remember with now, and Willa's e-mails were full of news about some guy named Doug that Jenny had never even met.

Atta squirmed in her sleep and meowed irritably. When Jenny reached down to pet her, she touched the chrystal pendant that Nitty Gritty the Newfangler had hung on her collar. That was when they were in a whole other universe. In that entirely pale world, only Atta had kept her color. She was tremendously admired in the White World, where nobody had ever seen color before. But Terran Tuhlla the Terrible and his grim Ghanglers didn't admire her a bit. They wanted everything and everyone to conform to their rigid White World rules. They *hated* color, even though, like everyone else on that planet, they'd never seen it. They'd only felt it in the works of the marvelous Chrystellean masterworkers, and they'd proclaimed that all Ghanglers were forbidden to even touch those works.

Then Jennifer, Willa, and Atta Girl had been dropped into the White World, where even the two girls were all white, leaving behind Jenny's red hair and freckles and Willa's warm, chocolate complexion. But Atta Girl had somehow managed to arrive with the hue of her gorgeous marmalade-colored fur and her glowing yellow eyes intact, so of course the Ghanglers super-hated Atta Girl. The Ghangler whirlies despised Jenny and Willa too, since, even though they were also all white on this world, the girls were subtly different from the White Worlders, especially in what they wore.

Jennifer had quit trying to tell Mom and Dad about the White World. She did try at first, but then Mom would get that worried crease in the middle of her forehead when she looked at her, and Dad would look up from his book or newspaper when he thought Jennifer wasn't noticing and shake his head sadly. She couldn't really blame them. If it hadn't happened to her, she wouldn't have believed it either.

But at least there was Warren, her eleven-year-old brother. He loved to listen from the beginning. He'd sit in the wooden rocking chair in her room with his legs pulled up tightly beneath him. He particularly liked hearing about all the close calls they'd had with the ghoulish Ghanglers and the time Jenny was nearly killed by a storming star and Morgan the Wonderful, Wandering Wohtt had saved her life. Warren liked to sit and shiver with dread from his safe distance. But Jenny didn't think he actually believed her as much as he wanted to.

"We're on our way, Jennifer." Mom poked her head in the open door of Jenny's room to say good-bye. "Are you sure you can't go with us?"

"I'd like to, Mom. But I've got to get this science assignment done for tomorrow morning. Give them hugs for me, okay?"

Dad leaned over Mom's shoulder and winked at his daughter. "Hey, Funnyface," he said. "Hit those books."

"Okay, Dad." She grinned back. "Right away!" One of Dad's favorite jokes was ordering Jenny to do things she was already doing.

"Well ..." Mom hesitated, that little worry crease showing on her forehead again. There Jenny was, in high school and practically a grown woman, and her parents still worried about letting her stay home alone, especially since she had tried telling them about the White World.

"Well," Mom repeated, "Warren will be with us, so you won't be disturbed. Call if you need anything."

Jenny was glad she wouldn't be disturbed. The house did feel a bit hollow and echoey after they'd gone, though. She focused back on the chapter on dimensions in her science book. Knowing what weird tricks time can play doesn't mean you understand it—any more than you could understand the part in the book that explained, "In the fifth dimension, a cube would have countless corners."

"Hey," she muttered disgustedly to herself, "if it had all those corners, it wouldn't *be* a cube—would it?"

And there was the part of the lesson that told about a theory that there really isn't any gravity; it's just matter making space bend around Earth. It also said if the atoms in something got mashed horrifically close together it would be *ginormously* heavy, *and* it would wrap space around it so hard that it would suck everything nearby right into it. *Like black holes and,* she supposed, *maybe white holes. Or maybe white holes would do the opposite, like blow everything away?* But Jenny didn't believe that because she already knew something about white holes and how they behaved. And she couldn't see *why* she needed all this other stuff. Now that she was back home, all she'd ever need to know about time was how to read clocks and calendars and how to know which way was up or down or right or left, for pity's sake.

Outside some kids were playing one-on-one in the street, and a car door slammed. The outside noises made the inside of the house seem even emptier. Jenny stretched her mind through all the empty rooms, enjoying having the house to herself.

Scritt! Something automatic turned on or turned off. Jennifer put her chin in her hands and stared blankly at the hungry hippo stain on her wallpaper where she'd knocked over her paint water a few summers ago. Back when she was in the White World, she'd been afraid she'd never see this room with that silly hippo stain again.

Bong-bong-bong. The clock in the front hall—the one with the stars, moon, and sun chasing each other around a little window—chimed insistently. She sighed. She knew this much about time. If she didn't start this paper now, she'd never finish it on time.

Click-snick. The house settled its rafters around her aloneness, and Jennifer snuggled into it comfortably.

Then something ... something like a silver wind ... slipped warmly into the room to lift the hair from the nape of her neck. Even then she didn't have a clue about what was about to happen. There had been times when she'd known something was wrong ahead of time, times when she got all spooky and bristly and she didn't realize why until later. But that's the trouble with intuition—you can't count on it.

She shook her head and forced her eyes back to the lesson, but her mind would have nothing to do with it. There was a wrinkle in a corner of her paper where her elbow had leaned on it. She tried to smooth it with her fingers and then pulled out a fresh sheet from the desk drawer and started again: Jennifer Arthur, Science 1A, Novem—

Snick—crack—thwannng!

Jennifer gasped and Atta yowled as the air around them twisted violently. *Earthquake?* Jennifer thought, panicked. She'd lived all her life in Northern California where people were always talking about earthquakes, but she'd never actually felt one. And she was puzzled when she heard the game going on outside the same as before.

Then she heard something else through the crackling and sparking of the air around her. It sounded faintly like far-off chimes, like a distant doorbell rung by welcome visitors. Her mind reached back. Where *had* she heard those chimes before?

Jennifer shook her head to clear it. *It definitely was an earthquake,* she decided. *It had to be. What had happened when the chimes had sounded before was something gentle and easy, not wild like this. Besides, that had happened in a whole other universe and it could not ... possibly ... be ... happening ... again.*

She stayed sitting on the floor of her room for a minute, rubbing the place on her arm where she'd bumped it against her desk when she fell. Things were settling down, but Atta's back fur was still ruffled, and Jenny's heart was still pounding.

The air smoothed around them, though, and the spitting, sparking static that had come with the scary, crumpling air faded to nothing. *It was an earthquake*, Jennifer decided again as she looked around. Even though everything was exactly as it had been before, her mind insisted it had to have been at least a tremor. Even though her stuffed animals were still tossed together on her bed in the same positions, and her bulletin board still hung straight on the wall. And even the things pinned to it—a party invitation, a picture of her and Willa grinning and squinting at the sun, and a metal T square—didn't look any more crooked than before. Her hot pink alarm clock told her it was 3:11 p.m. It hadn't missed a tick.

"No harm done," she told Atta, her voice coming out strange and cracked. "This is earthquake country, you know," she said proudly, as if it were something brave and special to live their lives on that slippery section of the planet.

Outside, the game was over, and skateboarders were doing stunts in driveways, but that was all. There were no sirens or unusual noises. The phone wasn't ringing, either, so Mom and Dad probably hadn't even felt it. *It would just be something to talk about in school Monday*, she thought.

"Did you feel the earthquake yesterday?"

"Yeah, did you?"

"Where were you when it hit?"

Jenny pulled herself up, set her chair upright, and then sat in it again, squarely in front of her desk. The excitement was over. She wasn't trembling because she was still scared, she told herself. It was only that she hadn't stopped shaking yet. *This was normal. This was California. This was now.* She picked her paper and pen up off the floor where they'd fallen, placed them on the desk side by side, and jumped a foot when an envelope appeared just a few inches in front of her nose.

Its pearly paper and silver lettering shimmered in the afternoon light as it floated over her desk. She couldn't believe her eyes.

"No, Atta," she said firmly, as if her cat had been arguing with her. "No, it can't be from Nitty." *How could Nitty Gritty Newfangler just drop them a note, all the way from another universe?* Atta sprang up into Jenny's lap to see what her mistress was carrying on about.

"See here, though, Atta?" Still not touching it, Jenny pointed out the silvery writing on the envelope. "It's addressed to all of us—to you, to me and to Willa. Oh, if only Willa were here now!" She was beginning to let her excitement loose. She remembered the chimes and began to let herself believe.

"Maybe—maybe it wasn't an earthquake after all, Atta." It was hard on Jenny that Atta couldn't answer her anymore. *And it must be terrible,* she realized suddenly, *for Atta Girl!* Absently, she rubbed the favorite furry place behind her cat's ears, still puzzling things out as the wonder of it washed over her. She whispered then, as if to speak out loud might break the spell. She wouldn't rush this. It would be like unwrapping a package that you're sure holds exactly what you want, but unwrapping it slowly, a ribbon here, a piece of tape there—folding the paper carefully and setting it aside before opening the box, to make the lovely expectation last.

Impatiently, Atta butted her head against Jenny's hand, demanding she get on with it. The girl's hands were damp with excitement, and she rubbed them on her jeans before she reached to touch the envelope. It dropped into her hand as if it belonged there, and Jenny supposed it did.

She opened it carefully. "It is! It's from Nitty Gritty," she squeaked. "Oh Atta, a note from Nitty, all the way from the White World." She'd have known it was from Nitty when she read it, even without the sprawly silver signature at the bottom. It was written in Nitty's own mixture of Pilgrim English and outdated slang:

> Methinks 'twould be a zowie treat,
> If the three of thee—and we—should meet.
> We'll kick up our heels and have a hoedown,
> Then rest, and catch up on the lowdown.
> We'll chat about now and of days gone by,
> When the three of thee came from out of the sky.
> If thou'lt choose to be there (thou'lt not be sorry)
> Then go today, and not tomorry,
> To stand beside your lilac tree.
> Then wait right there 'til half past three.

"She's coming to see us, Atta! I don't know how it's possible, but she *is* clever." Atta purred and rubbed against her, as excited as she was. "It says for us to wait by the lilac tree, Atta. *Today* at 3:30. Oh, whoa! It's 3:18 already!"

Scooping Atta up, she rushed outside, careening through the narrow hallway, the crowded dining room, the tidy kitchen and the cluttered porch. The back door squawked a protest as she yanked it open and squealed a warning as it closed behind her.

Jenny didn't even slow down. Who pays attention to screen doors anyway?

Chapter 2

◆

Waiting

Jennifer was nearly to the lilac bush when she stopped abruptly. She and Atta Girl were the only ones there. Well, the note said three thirty. "There are still a few minutes to go," she said out loud.

"And Nitty said 'we,' Atta. Maybe Morgan will be with her." She grinned, remembering the soft, starry fluff that covered their Wohtt friend from head to hips, the silver bells that tipped his delicate antennae, his squared-off spectacles, his super fancy way of talking, and his plain, comfortable way of being a friend. "Or maybe Ildirmyrth the Masterworker," she went on, guessing out loud. "Or even Behrrn!" Her heart flip-flopped at that thought. "He probably can't leave Chrystellea, though," she cautioned Atta. "His people need him there." She didn't want to get Atta's hopes, or her own, up too high.

She put Atta on the ground and began to pace back and forth, making plans. Atta headed for her favorite spot on the back fence. "We'll serve them pizza, Atta," Jenny exclaimed, waving her hands excitedly. "We'll order out for pizza with everything. I'll bet they have never tasted anything like pepperoni pizza!"

Atta seemed unimpressed, and Jennifer was beginning to feel anxious. *It must be three thirty by now,* she worried. *Where are they?*

"And you know how Nitty loves gadgets," she babbled, trying not to worry. "We'll show her the television and my smartphone. Won't she be interested?" Then she laughed at herself. Nitty Gritty the Newfangler was a lady who'd invented all kinds of things, even a way to send notes across universes. Why would she be impressed with appliances? After all, it wasn't as if Jenny herself had invented the telephone or anything else. About all she herself knew, Jenny realized, was how to use these things—how to turn them off and on.

There was one thing about Earth that would totally bowl them over, though—the color! Color everywhere! All they had in the White World was a *memory* of color, built into their artworks. And, before Jennifer, Willa and Atta Girl had arrived there, the people of that world had almost lost that.

"Oh, Atta," she said as she looked in all the corners of the yard. "I can't wait to introduce them to Mom and Dad. And Warren will turn inside out with excitement!" She went over to paw through the leaves of the lilac bush as if their friends might be hiding in it, somehow. She realized how dumb that was, though. The bush was bigger than it had been when the white hole had rolled right up to it—the hole that had yanked the three of them clear to the White World—but it was definitely still not big enough for anyone to hide in.

And why would they hide from me, anyway? Jennifer began pacing again. Waiting was not one of the things she did best.

"Do you suppose they'll be able to stay long enough to visit school with me?" she wondered aloud, standing still just long enough to turn around and around like a lighthouse lantern so she wouldn't miss them when they came. She just couldn't admit to herself that they might not make it after all. When she remembered the movie *ET* and how the scientists in it had reacted to the knowledge that a real live alien was on Earth, she decided that a school visit might not be such a great idea after all.

Even so, she giggled as she pictured Morgan strolling down the wide, waxed, high school halls, shedding soft dandelion-type fluff along the way. The kids would have to pick their jaws up off the floor.

But even with allowing for her clock to have been a few minutes fast, where were they? Jenny began to feel foolish, rushing into her backyard to look for aliens. Maybe she *had* been imagining things. For reassurance, she reached down to touch the chrystal pendant Nitty Gritty had hung on Atta girl's collar.

Then suddenly, without a breath of warning, she and Atta Girl were somewhere else. Last time there had been the wild trip through the white hole, misty, scary, and vague. This time there was nothing between worlds. Nothing at all, except—like when you're riding in a fast train through a dark forest and suddenly there's a house ahead, with a lighted window you want to see into. You absolutely yearn to see who lives there, and whether they're washing dishes or reading or playing cards—but then you're beyond it already, and you'll never know who lived there.

Or what.

Chapter 3

◆

Nobody Home

And that's how it was, a blink between, and they were on the other side.

Jenny'd landed in one of Nitty's comfy, musically operated chairs with Atta on her lap. She ran her fingers over the wooly-feeling upholstery fabric, testing its reality. Her heart pounded with excited anticipation.

After she could breathe again, Jennifer whispered in her cat's ear. "Atta, we're *here* in Nitty Gritty's very own house in the side of the mountain. Oh Atta, somehow, some way, *we've* come to the White World to visit *them!*" Jenny hugged Atta tightly, trying to adjust to this different reality. It took a while to completely focus her eyes and her mind to that colorless world again. Just like the first time, everything on the White World was completely white, or silver, or colorless, even her own skin, her red hair, her clothes, her freckles, *everything* except, as before, Atta Girl was as ginger-orange as ever.

Jenny felt a small pang of regret. This time, she'd like to have come as *she* really was too, with her own red hair—sun-sprinkled freckles and all. But she adapted, without her setting off her quick temper. Most people blamed her temper on her red hair. She'd been working *hard* on that part, and doing well, she thought. She'd vowed to never "pop off" again.

Jenny's excitement grew as she began to notice little things she remembered. There was the ceramic white owl sitting on the top of the amazing corner cupboard; there were the small arched doors where

15

Nitty's musically propelled furniture was garaged. Over on the other side of the rock-carved room, curly beakers, petri dishes, and other scientific stuff were stacked everywhere on the long counter next to the big, claw-legged stove. Then there was a soft tinkling sound, and a movement caught her eye. It made her smile as she recognized Nitty Gritty's fluttering chrystal butterfly, perched as always on one of Nitty's many bookshelves. In some places on the shelves, there were even books—thick, scientific books—written about a science which no way resembled the science Jenny studied in school.

"Everything looks exactly the same," she told Atta, "except for that big empty spot on the counter." Atta Girl purred in agreement. "When we were here before, the only empty spot anywhere was in that corner cupboard, remember?" The cupboard on which the ceramic white owl sat looked as empty as it did before. This time, though, Jenny already knew that the cupboard was a special place, a secret connection with Behrrn the Rememberer's country, the underground nation of Chrystellea.

Jenny shuddered as she wondered whether they were expected to go to Chrystellea to meet their friends. Much as she longed to return to that beautiful, friendly underground nation, she hoped she wouldn't need to go there by way of the mile-high stepping-stones, which were invisibly suspended high in midair. She was less afraid of heights than she used to be, but she couldn't forget the time she'd actually fallen off of one of the top stones; if she hadn't happened to fall onto another stepping-stone that spiraled below it on the way down ... well, it would have been the end of her, right there!

Chrystellea was a lovely place to visit but when they'd been there before, about all she and Willa could think about was how, and *if*, they would ever get home again. Anyway, if once she and Atta got themselves down those stairs this time, Chrystellea would be the best place to have a relaxed time and to really visit with their friends. She couldn't wait to catch up on everything that had happened since they left. Maybe it would even be interesting to do a little *careful* sightseeing on the planet's surface too.

They needed to be careful, because anywhere on the surface Tehrran Tuhlla the Terrible's Ghangler gangs might turn up through their creepy "power circles." It was only underground where Jenny and Atta Girl could feel truly safe.

They would be safe there, because Tuhlla the Terrible had never found Chrystellea, at least not while they were here before. This time, Nitty Gritty had also sent for them, and Jennifer knew that she would never, ever do that if she hadn't also figured out some way to get them home again.

In spite of their worries and close calls the last time, they'd had good times in Chrystellea. The citizens on the surface proved to be friendly and helpful too, except for the Ghanglers, of course. So there was a sweet gladness that came with being back. *This time,* Jennifer assured herself again, *that spooky Tuhlla and his Ghangler thugs wouldn't even know she and Atta were there.* She did miss Willa, though. *She'll be totally golly-green after she learns That Atta and I have visited here without her,* she realized. *If only she could have come too!*

She set Atta Girl down on the solid rock floor of the cave-house and stood up, looking around again for any sign of Nitty or any of their friends. Where were they? She began to pace, looking in doors and cupboards. You just never knew about doors and cupboards in Nitty's laboratory-home. *Why, though, wasn't the Newfangler there to meet them? Surely she'd have at least left a note!* Jenny examined the big room still more carefully, even looking under furniture and inside the furniture garages. Nitty's breakfast dishes were still on the table, as if she'd been called away in a hurry.

"She *must* have left a note," Jenny told Atta, trying to revive hope. She looked in even smaller places, searching again through Nitty's jolly jumble of things. Atta Girl even stretched her paw into a mouse hole to check if anything was in there.

Some of the clutter was new. There was a tiny white marble unicorn she hadn't seen on the last visit, a new lace fan, a silver-cat music box, and something that looked like a saxophone with ears but probably wasn't. Little things like that. What was the most different, though, was a wide, cleared-off place on one of the counters. Uncluttered space was something totally unexpected in Nitty's laboratory-parlor.

But it was the nobody-here feeling that was getting to Jenny. She was about to give up her search and think seriously about the corner cupboard and the stepping-stones-in-space just beyond them—*way down* to Chrystellea and hopefully to Behrrn. But just then she heard footsteps outside!

"Listen, Atta, somebody's coming at last!" She rushed to one of the small, arched front windows. Oh wow! It was Morgan Milceford Mandrake Morton Wilberforce Warner Wilhelm Woohane Killyburr Karlton Clarington Shane Brandywine Barrington Billereebott—Morgan the Wonderful, Wandering Wohtt. Dear, dear Morgan of the many names! He was hurrying eagerly up the path to Nitty's front door. His star-tipped fluff glimmered in the white light and his antennae jingled cheerily. When Jenny saw him, the little cave house became warm, welcoming, and cozy again, as it should be. She headed for the front door to meet him.

Waaaaait! Atta's warning slipped into her mind, but she had heard the ruckus too, so she didn't think about the fact that this was the first thing her cat had "said" since they'd arrived. Cautiously, she peeked out the window again, and what she saw made her have to fight to keep from falling headlong into the panic that opened like a pit inside her belly!

Ghanglers!

"Morgan!" she tried to call out, but her voice was choked with fear. "Oh, Morgan, look out!"

One of the eight-feet-tall Ghanglers came up behind the Wohtt as she watched. He moved swiftly on his own small, vicious whirlwind. Three more quickly appeared, all of them yelling and grabbing at Morgan. Jenny could only hear snatches of what they were saying … there was nothing that made sense, only clicking, growling sounds—not words. It took a while, she remembered, to adapt to Ghangler talk.

She called out to Morgan again as she raced back to open the door for him, but he couldn't have heard her over the Ghanglers' shouting, even if her voice had been working properly.

Even more Ghanglers appeared out of what seemed like nowhere. Jenny looked around the laboratory-parlor quickly. What could she use as a weapon? Was there even a rock she might throw? Terror flooded through her as their raucous, spiteful voices and the sound of their angry, hissing whirlwinds filled the air, even inside the Newfangler's cave. Cold sweat coated her forehead as she peeked cautiously through the lacy curtains. The Ghanglers were *so* tall, and Morgan wasn't even as tall as Jenny. *And oh! There were so many of them shouting at him!* They brutally knocked him to the ground, and then yanked him up, so they could push him down again.

Morgan didn't appear to speak at all. It was as if he knew it was no use. When he saw how many there were he simply stayed on the ground where they had thrown him. He had a patient, slightly sad expression on his dandelion-like fluffy face. One of the Ghanglers fastened heavy cuffs to his slender, downy wrists and used the chains attached to them to yank him to his feet again.

Frantically Jennifer ran back and forth between the door and the window, trying to think of something, anything, she could do.

The Ghanglers shoved the Wohtt out in front of them then and started to move away. "Oh, Morgan," Jennifer wailed again as Atta Girl mewled and growled. "I just can't let them take you!" But she knew that if she ran out there the Ghanglers would only snatch her and Atta Girl too. Then nobody would know what happened to any of them!

The one with his hand resting heavily on one of Morgan's shoulders turned suddenly for a last look in the direction of Nitty's front door. Jenny pulled away from the small arched window in the door window quickly, but not before she saw the Ghangler's nose, a nose that seemed to slice an opening in his taller-than-his-head collar, and not before she glimpsed those cruel, pale eyes, like uncooked oysters. It was not before she turned cold with terror. And it was not before she recognized— Terran Tuhlla the Terrible *in person!*

Jennifer leaned her head against the cold window grid, watching Tuhlla lead his Ghangler gang away from Nitty's front door, with Morgan a prisoner in the middle of them. Since she'd been back on Earth again, she'd sometimes seen the Terrible Tuhlla in her nightmares. But seeing him in real life again—that was a zillion times worse; she was trembling so hard her teeth rattled.

As she watched helplessly, the brutal whirlwind-walkers yanked Morgan off his feet and shoved him back and forth between them. They held him dangling from the chains and then dropped him to the ground before yanking him back up so they could knock him around still more. Jennifer forgot to be careful about being seen as she watched, but it didn't matter. The monsters were too busy getting their fun, all of them against one small, fluffy Wohtt. If only there was something she could use as a weapon! She glanced quickly around Nitty's parlor again before turning back to the window. Her eyes got hot and dry with the strain, but she blinked back her tears and kept watching. She was frightened, helpless, frustrated, and *furious.*

Several yards from Nitty's cave house, the Ghanglers who were tormenting Morgan met other Ghanglers coming. They were hauling an empty sled. These Ghanglers were huffing and puffing as if the sled were made of lead, and loaded with it too. Tuhlla the Terrible threw one of the tow ropes over Morgan's frail shoulder, and gestured that he should get up and help pull it. Jenny knew that, as he tugged, the rope would quickly wear a huge bald spot in his delicate, starry fluff. But his fluff was falling out right and left anyway, as it always did when he was stressed.

The Ghanglers headed for a circle of stiff, fake-looking bushes. It was obviously one of their sneaky power circles. Jenny remembered the habit they had of appearing anywhere on open ground, through the centers of those flower-bordered tornadoes. The circles appeared wherever the girls and Atta went on the White World except in the underground, island nation of Chrystellea, and even there, sometimes. The circles of stiff plants or cutout-looking blooms grew up and spread out as the grinding tornadoes chewed up everything in their centers. The footless Ghanglers used the power of the whirlwind, similar to the small whirlwinds they moved around on.

Just before they entered the waiting power circle, though, Morgan suddenly dropped the tug rope. At the same time he slipped out of the metal cuffs which were much too large for his slender wrists and moved toward the sled suddenly, as if trying to make a last-ditch escape. Then everything rippled around the scene, like heat rising on a desert highway.

When it cleared, the chains and manacles that had been fastened to his wrists were scattered on the ground, and Morgan was nowhere to be seen. All she saw were the Ghanglers acting excited, waving their scrawny arms wildly as they slithered back and forth.

Tuhlla's whirlwind rose and sparked around him. He shouted at the others so loudly that Jenny could almost understand the words, even from where she stood inside the cave. She was just as glad she couldn't, though, because the fearful cringing of the other Ghanglers made it clear that they weren't nice words at all.

After a few minutes of this, all of them moved into the still-growing power circle, cowering as Tuhlla followed. Small lightning bolts from his own whirlwind lashed painfully at any of them within reach.

Then they were gone.

"Why?" Jenny yelled at poor Atta Girl when she finally turned from the window. "Why did this happen? Ghanglers never bothered Morgan before!"

Atta stared back but didn't answer. When Jenny was scared she tended to get cranky, and her cat was aware that a quick answer wasn't a good idea.

"Why did the Ghanglers take Morgan after all this time?" her mistress added. "After all, they don't *know* how special he is, unless— unless someone told them!"

When they'd been on the White World before, the Ghanglers didn't know that Morgan was the only Wohtt known to be in existence. The genial Wohtt had convinced them, in that gentle way of his, that there were simply caboodles of Wohtts, all *exactly* alike but with different names. And that was just the way Tuhlla the Terrible liked things, all exactly alike. They never suspected that Morgan was all of those names.

But now they had taken him away, and who knew *what* they would do to him!

Jenny didn't notice when her tears started. They just slid down her face as if she had nothing to do with them. When she realized they were running off her chin, she wiped her hand across her face and then crossed her arms and stamped her foot, hard! She was entirely too angry to cry, she told herself. She stomped back and forth across the room yelling, from one mountain-rock wall to another.

She shuddered then, recalling that Nitty's little home was actually a cave, the only cave she'd ever liked in her whole life, and she was beginning to feel uneasy about this one. It was reassuring, though, to remember that Ghanglers could not penetrate solid rock with their power circles.

Atta Girl watched Jenny with wary yellow eyes and kept a safe distance. Although she knew Jenny would never harm her, it always bothered Atta to see her mistress cry or yell, and right then she was doing both.

"Morgan is so loyal and loving and brave!" Jenny wailed. "That is more than I can say about *me. He* was the one in trouble just now—terrible trouble—and what did I do? Nothing, that's what I did. I just hid here and watched it happen, that's what I did."

Whhaaaat coullld youuuu hhhave donnnne? her cat dared to ask.

"I—I don't know—but I should have done something!"

Wwwoould it haaave hellllped himmm if yyyyooou'd runnn out therrrre annnd got usssss bothhh caught wwwwith himmmm? Thennn nnnnobody wwwould knowww whaaaat happennned to himmm. Or to usssss.

Jenny had no answer for that, so she changed the subject. "When Nitty gets here she'll know what to do, won't she, Atta? Oh no!" The tear-streaked girl stopped pacing; she was struck by a new and dreadful thought. "Oh, Atta! Maybe the Ghanglers have Nitty too, because otherwise she'd have been here to meet us, wouldn't she?"

She began pacing again, diagonally across the room this time, because that gave her a longer pacing distance. She was thinking, hard. "They would have taken Morgan, and Nitty too if they have her, to Mimeopolis." Mimeopolis was the Ghanglers' creepy capital city. "If we can get hold of some of the invisibility whillyflowers, we can go look for them there."

They'd discovered the marvelous whillyflowers when they'd first come to the White World. That was when the white hole in space had rolled right through Jenny's back yard, swept them up, and deposited them there.

"And Behrrn! Behrrn will help us!" Jenny was on her way to the corner cupboard and to Behrrn, when the front door opened.

Chapter 4

Nitty Newfangler

"Jennifer Arthur!" Nitty Gritty exclaimed as she came into her laboratory-home. "Prithee," she asked in her sweet, throaty voice, "is it truly thee, Jennifer? Verily, I didst not expect thee till the morrow!"

Jenny had no sooner recognized the Newfangler that she was hug-deep in Nitty's personal fragrance, a special combination of fresh meadow breezes, silky talcum powder, and ... a pinch of vanilla, maybe. Something like that, only better.

"Oh Nitty," she wailed, "I thought the Ghanglers had taken you too."

"Taken me?" she repeated, pulling back to look at Jenny. "Golly gee whillikers, Jennifer—tears?" She touched a slender finger to a tear that still wobbled on Jenny's cheek. "Why wouldst the evil Ghanglers *take me* anywhere?"

"Well, they took Morgan. I *saw* them take Morgan."

"Art thou certain, Jennifer?" the Newfangler exclaimed in alarm. "Morgan?"

"Yes. Atta Girl and I saw them do it. He was coming up the path to your house, and the Ghanglers popped out of nowhere. You know how they do. I thought they must have taken you too. I thought that was why you weren't here to meet us when we came."

"Oh gosh, Jenny, how sorry I am that I was not. I truly blew it this time." Her forehead creased with puzzlement. "But verily, as I said,

I didst *not* expect thee until the morrow. I must have goofed in my calculations. 'Tis grieved I am that thou didst arrive without welcome." She bustled about the cave room as she spoke, setting water to boil for blumbutton tea on her huge stove, and pulling wall levers to bring two cushy, marshmallow-white chairs humming out through their respective small, arched doors. The arched doors lined one wall, and Jenny remembered that besides chairs, cloud-soft beds hummed out of them too, when they were needed.

Nitty urged Jennifer to relax in one of the chairs, and then she flopped into the other and leaned her head back wearily.

"Oh Nitty, don't worry about not being here," Jenny assured her. "You're here now, and we can just go get some whillyflowers and bring Morgan right back."

"Bring him back? Bring him back from where, Jenny? Dost thou know where the monsters have taken our dear Wohtt?"

"The Ghanglers take their prisoners to Mimeopolis, don't they?" Jenny asked eagerly. She figured they needed to get started. They needed to get some of the invisibility whillyflowers from Chrystellea and get going. She'd watched Morgan getting knocked around by the gruesome Ghanglers, and the very idea of Morgan as another of Tehrran Tuhlla's slaves was *way* too awful to imagine.

The Newfangler leaned forward to take Jenny's hands in hers. She looked at the girl earnestly, and as Jenny looked back at her, she noticed something that alarmed her even more. Even though Nitty still wore the same kind of open, sheer white lab coat as she had before over her T-shirt and white jeans, the T-shirt didn't sparkle with cheery messages anymore. Thinking back, Jenny realized it hadn't been sparkling from the time Nitty came in the door. Now it was simply dull, and all the T-shirt had to say for itself was, "GONE."

"Jenny dear, things have been changing here, ever since six storm cycles ago. Since that time, the whillyflower patrol in Mimeopolis has found no new slaveholding offenses, within that city." She paused, her eyes glazed over with pain and concern, and then she went on. "Nonetheless, there *hath* been disappearances during that time. Mostly disappearances of children, many of them. The little ones may, of course, have simply wandered off as children sometimes do. If so, they will surely soon be found." She continued, the stress in her voice tightening as she recalled *all* of the many disappearances of children that had occurred in the short time since she set the coordinates to bring Jenny, Willa, and Atta Girl back to the White World for a fun visit.

She shook her head slightly as if to clear it. "Willa didst not come with thee? Well," she went on, before Jenny could explain about Willa moving to Southern California, "it's just as well. Verily, something fearful is happening here, so I'll need to get you and Atta back home, right away. If the Ghanglers stole Morgan, there is no telling what they may be up to now or where they are hiding their victims." She raised a hand to brush a wisp of platinum hair from her forehead. "If only I had thought to cancel thy trip before thee came," she said worriedly. "What a bummer! It's obviously much too dangerous for thee and Atta Girl to be visiting now."

She stood up, pulling herself together with an obvious effort. "I must set the coordinates on the Chrystal Gate to return thee to thy home immediately. Atta and thee are not safe on the White World at this time. I truly goofed things up to call thee here, at a time like this."

"Oh no!" Jennifer protested. "We can't leave now. We haven't had any time to visit, and we can't possibly leave while Morgan is in such trouble. We've got to help him!"

Shaking her head sadly, Nitty turned away from her guests and toward the long, empty counter. When she saw its emptiness, though, she let out a choking scream. "'Tis gone!" she wailed. She turned back toward Jenny and Atta, fluttering her hands over her face as if she was deeply ashamed. "The Ghanglers must have stolen the Chrystal Gate, as well as our dear friend Morgan. I must have neglected to lock my door. I should have remained here with it, but the children—I *had* to help look for them, and I didst not expect thee until the morrow."

Jennifer's mouth went dry with dread. Nitty had always been in control; she had always been a capable, "in charge" person. It frightened her to see the Newfangler so upset. She grabbed the young woman's shoulders and shook them gently to get her attention and hopefully to stop the dreadful worry in her eyes.

"What is a Chrystal Gate, Nitty?" she asked urgently. "What is it that's gone?"

"Thy way back home to thy lovely, colorful Earth," Nitty sighed. "Thy only way!"

Chapter 5

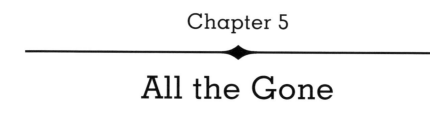

All the Gone

Jennifer's mind stalled for a long moment as she tried to understand what Nitty Gritty was telling her. She got the fact that a chrystal, half of something Nitty called a Chrystal Gate, had disappeared from Nitty's laboratory, most likely only moments before Jenny and Atta had arrived … just before she and Atta had found themselves in Nitty's Cave, and just before Morgan the Wonderful, Wandering Wohtt had come down the path.

Then the Gruesome Ghanglers had Wohtt-napped him, right before their eyes.

But she was still confused. What did that have to do with how she and Atta would get home again? Last time they were here, they'd managed to latch onto the white hole that brought them here. They'd caught it as it was beginning the shorter lap of the figure eight–shaped orbit, but this time she already knew that the white hole's long segment of the figure-eight orbit would not return for nearly a hundred years.

"If only I had at least corrected the gate's setting for your arrival. Verily, in that way the theft, at least, would be somewhat less of a disaster" Nitty wailed. 'Tis obviously much too dangerous here now, for thee and for Atta Girl. I blew it all to pieces this time, Jenny! I am a total goof-up!"

She wrung her hands in distress, looking around her cave room as if a solution might appear if she looked hard enough.

Okay, Jenny thought. The Chrystal Gate was how she and Atta had come back to the White World, specifically to Nitty's little home-laboratory-cave in the mountainside. And it appeared to be how she planned to send them home again after their visit.

"Okay," she said to Nitty reassuringly. "But since you're the one who made the Gate in the first place, you can just make another one, can't you?"

But at that, Nitty got even more agitated, sitting down, jumping up again, and moving jerkily around the room. She was so upset by this time that the ashy-looking message on her T-shirt seemed to actually smoke. At first the smell of smoke reminded Jenny of cinnamon toast, but it quickly began to smell more like *burned* cinnamon toast. Jenny was distracted as she watched this process; she feared the shirt might actually burst into flame and she lost track of what the Newfangler was telling her, until she heard Nitty exclaim, "the chrystal that I did use was one of only two ever found here on the White World," Her hands trembled as she steepled them together. "'Tis believed they must have struck our world as fragments of a small meteor from another universe. Oh, stupid, Nitty," she scolded herself, hitting her forehead with the heel of her hand as she paced around the room; picking things up; and looking behind, around, and under them. She checked all of her laboratory utensils, a pot holder in the shape of a blumbutton, and even the chrystal butterfly, as if either Morgan or the Chrystal Gate might be hiding under them. "Oh, dumb, dumb, *dumb!*"

The other chrystal, she explained as she searched, was the pendant that she'd hung on Atta Girl's collar during their first visit. "The two chrystals, I hoped, would then become contact points between thy world and ours, Jenny. I never told thee of my hopes when thou wert here because I was not certain that their properties would prove powerful enough to span the galactic void between us." She stopped pacing long enough to hit her forehead again. "Dumb, dumb, dumb me!"

She looked straight at Jenny as she finished. "As you see, it has taken many storm cycles to complete the process."

"Hmm. That might explain why Atta has been acting so strangely lately. And it could be the reason for the crack in our garage wall; the crack with the pearly paper in it."

"Verily," Nitty answered humbly. Jenny felt sure that if this universe had color in it, Nitty Gritty would be blushing like a beet. "Thy garage wall was an early miscalculation. I am deeply repentant about the damage, and I shall surely find some way to compensate thy parents for it. That is, I shall do so if—no *when*—we find the larger chrystal! At any rate, the coordinates were set more than seven moon orbits ago. When those dirty Ghangler crooks stole the gate, it must have jarred the settings, bringing thee here before expected."

"Wait a minute, Nitty!" Jenny gasped as sweat beaded suddenly on her forehead. "If Atta Girl is wearing the other chrystal, and she's here now, then there's no Chrystal Gate still on Earth to be our contact point, is there?"

Nitty moved abruptly to her claw-footed stove. She seemed to have decided suddenly that her visitors were hungry and that she needed to feed them immediately. She spooned a stew of some sort from a milky white bowl into a pewter-like container, and set it on the stove. With a cheery melody, fire leaped up beneath it. Jenny recalled that Nitty made great blisterberry stew. The Newfangler gave it a halfhearted stir then turned back to Jenny and Atta Girl. The cat, as gorgeously colorful as ever, was curled comfortably on Jenny's lap. "No, Jennifer, the fact that Atta's chrystal is here with her doth not create the problem. At least, 'tis not *the* problem. The problem is what should have been the solution. That is, since thou and Atta Girl didst step into the contact point that triggered thy transport here, the contact point by your lilac bush hath existed there as fully as it doth on our White World, and the other half of it, the larger half, is now somewhere *here*, on the White World."

Jenny noticed that the stew was about to boil over, so she put Atta down to dash over and lower the flame. The stove, however, had already sensed the problem. With one soft, warm tone, the fire diminished to a low glow. Since she was already there at the stove, Jenny stirred a few times while she considered Nitty's explanation.

"So now there are two chrystals, which, working together, make up a sort of intergalactic bridge," Jenny said thoughtfully as she stirred. "Is that right, Nitty?" She looked back over her shoulder at the Newfangler. "One of them is here, somewhere on the White World. We don't know where, but it's somewhere the Ghanglers are keeping it. And the other one is in my world, on Earth." Her pulse pounded so loudly in her ears, and in her throat, that she had to wait a long moment before she could continue. "And *that* one opens up right next the lilac bush, in my family's own back yard?"

Nitty seemed to shrivel with shame, as she lamented:

> I goofed a lot! Oh woe! Oh woe!
> I under-guessed our wicked foe.
> Oh evil day—I've lost the way,
> why could I not have let you stay
> there in your colorful, love-filled home,
> and just let well enough alone?!
>
> Oh woe, oh me! Oh golly gee!
> There's no excuse for flub-up me.
> But this it is that makes me grieve:
> I *brought* thee here, with no way to leave.
>
> And where, oh where have the Ghanglers got
> Our super-duper friend, the Wohtt.
> And another thing we've *got* to know
> Is, where didst our precious children go?
>
> Oh, I goofed up bad. I brought thee here,
> And now thou art stranded, Jenny dear.

"Oh no!" Jennifer protested. "That wasn't such a bad thing, at all. If we *hadn't* been here, we wouldn't have seen the Ghanglers kidnap Morgan. No one would know what happened to him!" For just a moment,

Jenny hesitated over the thought that if she herself didn't get home, no one there would ever know what happened to her, either. But she was here right now. "We can't possibly leave while Morgan is in such trouble. We've got to help him, and help find all the others who are gone too!" She turned away from her stirring so suddenly that a chair near to her rolled back a few feet, humming a rather alarmed little melody.

Jennifer Arthur was ready to join the hunt.

Chapter 6

◆

The Hunters and
the Hunted

Meanwhile in Mimeopolis, white mists coiled and twisted in the fields outside and through its city streets. There, inside the city walls, they writhed with an eerie, voodoo-like movement and rhythm. The fogs there didn't just drift, veiling and dimming the look of things; these white mists seemed to erase whatever they passed in front of. And they were everywhere, drifting in and out of the glassless windows and doors whenever they opened. It made whole buildings appear to be suspended in air, only to rest again on terra firma as the mists moved on. Merchants' carts might disappear with only their goods suspended invitingly until the fog moved and erased the merchant or the customers' heads instead.

Inside the Imperial Tower the fog seemed more agitated than usual, creating a white-on-white strobe light effect inside the halls. Especially in Terran Tuhlla the Terrible's Imperial Office—the office at the very top of the tower, the only room there.

Tuhlla and his officers flickered in the mists as he outlined the next steps in his particularly vicious plan to subjugate all of the White World by kidnapping the citizens' children. "Parents whose children are held hostage," Tuhlla explained, "will not dare to rebel. Meanwhile, we Ghanglers will have a perfect opportunity to train the children from the beginning. It will be the ideal opportunity to teach them from the start about the beauty *and lawfulness* of our completely conforming Ghangler society."

Suddenly an ominous wind howled through the room, clearing the mists from it for a moment—but only for a moment. They flowed back into the room even more whipped up than before. Tuhlla broke off in the middle of a sentence and raised his head as if listening to a sudden, sour sound or smelling an unpleasant odor.

"Wait!" he roared, holding out his long, bony hand to silence the muttering that had begun with the interruption. "They are back! The earthling aliens have returned! At least the, ugh, feline alien is here, somewhere. I feel it! I feel it now! I *feel* its ghastly color!" Tuhlla's personal whirlwind rose up thickly through the mists that swirled around him and up to his scrawny neck. It left only his sharp-nosed face visible, tucked inside of his ridiculously high collar and poking through a flickering halo of small, fierce lightning bolts. The personal whirlwinds of the Ghanglers nearest to him puckered and shrank beneath them, and those Ghanglers who could, moved fearfully back out of the range of Tuhlla's electrified fury.

"Noooo!" Tuhlla shrieked as the mist thinned again to reveal even more clearly his ghastly features. "It's gone!" His collar pulled clear away from his head and drooped over his shoulders. He lowered his head for a moment as the mists began to settle toward his feet, revealing his long, straight-up-and-down gown and the whirlwind beneath that spat even larger and more deadly lightning bolts. But then the mists rose, straining to reach his shoulders, once again.

As Tuhlla's grim garment continued spitting at his officers, he said in a low and threatening voice, "It will return. And I shall have it for our White World Zoo Project. The bunch of you incompetent boobs lost the Wohtt for me, but we shall find him again, or another like him. And we will have those aliens in our Imperial Zoo, as well!" He laughed dreadfully at this thought, his uncooked-egg-white eyes unsmiling. Yes, we must prepare their cages ... *Now!*"

☆　　☆　　☆

Atta Girl walked daintily back into Nitty's cave room where Jennifer stood waiting for her, holding the heavy, arched door open just a cautious crack. She closed it with immense relief once her cat was inside again.

Atta had waited patiently for what seemed like very long minutes, facing the outside door like a dog on point. She had begun to squirm, and pleading thoughts entered Jennifer's mind before she noticed Atta and let her out. Jenny had forgotten to set up something she could use for a litter box. Silently, she apologized to Atta and, also silently, Atta forgave her.

"Oh, Atta and Jennifer dears," Nitty Gritty exclaimed as the cat settled down to groom herself. "I almost forgot that I have presents for both of thee, so both of thee canst go out-of-doors on the surface with little danger."

Jenny, Nitty, and Atta's other White World friends had first suspected and then became sure that somehow Tuhlla had been focusing on Atta Girl's colors, in order to locate them. But it was Jennifer who realized it first, and she worried the whole time they were in Chrystellea that the three of them were bringing danger to the kindly people of the underground nation.

The Ghanglers' sneaky power circles hounded them everywhere they went on that first visit, even sprouting up in Chrystellea, where they had never been seen before. The citizens, though, had formed power circle squadrons throughout the islands so they could spot, dig up, and bury any circles that appeared there. They didn't let them ripen enough to allow Ghanglers to enter through them in gardens or landscaping; the solid rock of the cavern also provided great protection.

Nitty Gritty reached into a drawer and pulled out two white, slouchy bags with tie handles. They were beautifully embroidered on all sides. "First, a gift for thee, Atta Girl." Atta's bag had silvery butterflies on it. Nitty laid it on Jenny's lap, next to Atta, and Jenny opened it carefully. Atta purred and sniffed it, as Jennifer looked doubtfully at the brush that was inside. Atta Girl always insisted that she took care of her own grooming, and she'd resisted brushing, although petting was always welcome. Although Atta's marmalade fur looked just fine, Jenny used the gift brush and began to brush her. Atta simply stretched out across

Jenny's lap and continued to purr. Neither Jenny nor Atta wanted to disappoint Nitty.

"What a lovely gift, Nitty." Jennifer tried to show the proper enthusiasm for the brush, but all that swirled in her brain were nightmare imaginings of power circles opening up in the middle of her unsuspecting family's backyard, and hordes of whirlwind-powered Ghanglers surrounding them, *completely* out of nowhere. She didn't really think that Ghanglers could conquer Earth, or the United States, or even California; but if Mom should go out into their back yard to water her flowers, or if Warren ran out there to play, or even if Dad should go out there with the garbage or to mow the lawn, well, there's no telling what awful things the Ghanglers might do. It would be the *worst!*

She remembered all too well when that orbiting white hole had dropped them on the White World. Soon after she, Willa, and Atta Girl had been dumped by the White Hole onto a wide, white field, the Ghanglers had popped out of a power circle nearby. They'd moved toward the girls almost soundlessly on their little whirlwinds. Her muscles had nearly turned to water at the sight of them,—eight feet tall or more and apparently footless. She recalled their creepy, bony fingers as they'd touched, pulled, and pinched Willa and herself on their faces, hair, and clothes.

As she remembered, she continued to brush Atta Girl. She wasn't thinking about that, only doing it. Suddenly she realized that wherever she brushed it, Atta Girl's fur turned a soft, silvery, platinum white.

"Oh, Nitty, this really *is* a fabulous gift! Now Atta can go outside here without calling the attention of the Ghanglers. Except for her yellow eyes …" She looked carefully at Atta Girl, and told her cat, "Squint a lot when you're on the surface, Atta. If you do, this brush should disguise you well enough to keep the Ghanglers off our trail!"

Ssssuperrrr! Atta answered, stretching out even more comfortably and then settling peacefully for more brushing.

Now, Jenny thought, *if only there were a way for them to block or destroy the Chrystal Gate on the Earth side.* Then, of course, she'd have no way to get home, ever, but at least her family would be safe.

ALICE SALERNO

She looked up. Nitty Gritty was talking to her.

"And there is but a short time left before the stars storm," she was saying. "I truly must rejoin the search for the children. Meanwhile Atta and thee will be safe in Chrystellea until I return."

"Before you go, Nitty," Jenny exclaimed desperately, "You wrote a note to me on Earth. Couldn't you write one to warn my family about the Ghanglers? That Ghanglers may be coming into our own backyard? *Couldn't you?*"

Reluctantly, the Newfangler explained that she would need the missing Chrystal Gate to boost the delivery of her notes to Earth. She could transmit notes to anywhere on the White World, but to reach another universe (Earth's, for instance) *both* of the chrystals were absolutely necessary.

Jennifer shuddered with dread for her family, then decided that they must, of course, get busy and *find* all of those who are gone— all the gone; Morgan, the children, and the other chrystal for the Chrystal Gate. She especially prayed that they would find and restore the gate before the Ghanglers learned to use it and invaded her family's backyard.

Nitty handed Jennifer the second bag—a gift for her. Focusing on it while hiding her worries from Nitty, Jenny touched the stitching on the bag, and as she felt the texture of its silver embroidery, she was startled to recognize her own dream dragon, dominant above the other dragons embroidered there. It was the very same dream dragon that had come to her when she was a prisoner in a Ghangler cell. That was the time when she was afraid that a prisoner of or slave for the "whooshers" was all she would ever be.

In an important way, it had been that very same dream dragon who had given her the key to her freedom. Smiling with the memory of that freedom-time, that going-home time, she opened the bag.

Inside was clothing like the girls and women wore on the White World. "'Thy jeans be greatly practical and truly *jazzy*, Jenny," Nitty confided. "That's why I wear similar garb. But when going about on the surface I dress more conservatively, for safety's sake. Where Ghanglers

36

roam, 'tis risky business to be different. Thou wilt not need such costuming in underground Chrystellea, of course."

Jennifer unfolded the first item out of her dragon bag. It was a full length dress, white of course, with some inconspicuous touches of silver. A cloud soft sweater was folded under it, and a finely knit shawl was beneath that. She held the shawl up and discovered that it draped beautifully, holding its shape however it was arranged. It would be helpful on the surface to drape it over her head, or across her face, when Ghanglers strolled nearby.

"Thanks loads, Nitty," she exclaimed sincerely. "Really, these will make things much safer and more comfortable when going about on the surface. But what's this?" Still in the box was something gleaming with diamond-like jewels. She held up the most beautiful gown she'd ever seen in her life, except maybe in movies. The sleeves were long and sheer, split from shoulder to wrist, and gathered at those wrists with sparkling bracelets. The bodice was fitted to a tiny waistline and the skirt was full and flowing. She wondered if it could possibly fit her. She just knew it would swirl beautifully if she was dancing, but where on Earth, *or* on the White World, would she wear it?

"That is for thee to wear at the party which is planned in honor of thy visit. The party will, of course, be delayed until all the gone are found, but for a surety there will be a grand party for thee and Atta Girl when our problems are resolved. And thou shalt surely wear it then."

Later, Nitty and Jennifer hurriedly finished the tasty limplilee salad and heffleroot stew that Nitty set out for them. She put a bowl of the stew on the floor for Atta Girl.

Jenny and Nitty were stacking the dishes in the sink when there was a frantic pounding on the cave's front door.

When Nitty opened it, a distraught couple nearly fell through it.

"Sahllee? Jeohff? What is it that distresses thee so?" Nitty asked.

"Oh Newfangler Dear, it's our babies! They're *gone!*"

"All three of them? *How?*"

"We don't know, Nitty," Jeohff moaned. "We knew that *so* many children had turned up missing, so we were watching our own so hard our eyes felt like they'd fall out. We put them to bed a short time ago, with all doors and windows locked shut. We went back only minutes later—and they were gone."

"How could that be?" Sahllee sobbed. "How could our babies just disappear?"

"I know not how that was, but I *doth* know that we shall find them." A flickering sparkle started on Nitty's T-shirt as the message rewrote itself to say, "LET'S GO!" She grabbed a cloak from a wall hook and pointed to the cloak that was hanging under it. "That one is thine, Jennifer. If thee hast to go on the surface at any time, remember that these cloaks will disguise you somewhat, and they also will protect you against storming stars. But for now, get thee quickly down to Chrystellea and wait there. I will contact you later!"

"But ..."

"To Chrystellea," Nitty ordered as she joined Sahllee and Jeohff by the outside door. And then, quite unlike herself, she demanded, *"Quickly!"*

Nitty and the frantic parents slipped out the door as Jenny stood there, wondering what to do next.

Goooo tooo Chryssstellea, came Atta's determined mind voice, *as Nnnnitty hassss dirrrected.*

"All right, all right!" Jenny blustered and then turned fearfully toward the corner glass cupboard. She had always been afraid of heights. Although that fear was somewhat conquered, she remembered all too well the terrifying stepping-stones-in-air that led to the underground nation.

Bracing herself, she picked up Atta Girl and stepped into the corner cupboard and out through its walk-through wall. On the other side, she stood trembling on the topmost of the stepping-stones-in-air, which spiraled down and down and down to the largest of the several islands in an underground sea.

Chapter 7

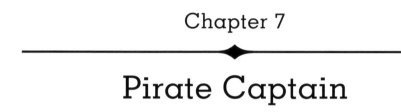

Pirate Captain

Quickly Jenny pulled her eyes up to look only ahead, before the distance below the stepping-stones-in-air could pull her down. Almost immediately, though, she realized that something was different about them. It was something new and wonderful! A softly glowing handrail wound down alongside the stones, adding a feeling of, well, almost security.

She set Atta on the stone beside her and grasped the railing. Comfort and a steady, confident feeling seemed to radiate from it. She took a grateful breath before stepping to the next stone and then the next. As she descended, she finally dared to look below to the lights of the Chrystellean buildings, which danced like fireflies, even sending flickering lights to the distant cavern walls. As she got closer, she saw a crowd gathering at the bottom of the stairway. The crowd made her a bit uneasy, but the handrail kept her anxiety under control, and when she realized that the people were cheering, and calling her and Atta's names, she was thrilled with the greeting.

Nakeesha, Chrystellea's Prime Minister, stood in front of the group holding her white porcelain rainbow-shaped staff. Although she had strongly opposed giving shelter to the earthlings the last time they were here, this time she moved toward Jenny and Atta Girl with a welcoming smile. After all, Jenny reminded herself, Nakeesha had risked her own freedom to enter the Ghangler capital of Mimeopolis in disguise to help her escape from the Grim Ghangler who had captured her in Mimeopolis and thrown her into his locked cellar. The prime minister came to her rescue right along with Behrrn and Nitty Gritty. That was when the way was opened for the three earthlings to run and leap into the orbiting white hole, which touched down right in the middle of Mimeopolis. That was their way to get home again.

Home. The sudden thought of home sent a flutter of anxiety through her, but she shook it off as much as she could. That figure eight orbit of the White Hole, she knew, would not be coming again for more than ninety-nine years.

Well, she'd deal with what was here for now and with getting home again when that time came. If it came.

Jennifer and Atta Girl stepped onto the island from the lowest stepping-stone and heard, for the first time, their new titles. They were hailed as heroes because of their part in helping Behrrn recall the Dream. Voices all around them were cheering for the Dreamsavers.

Behrrn's childhood dream of color had transformed the already beautiful Chrystellean masterworks, their artists and artisans absorbed his dream memory, and transferred the memory of color into their works. These works became the backbone of their economy and the heart of their morale. The masterworks had become valuable exports that enriched the lives of Chrystelleans and White Worlders everywhere.

Nakeesha almost smiled when she saw Atta Girl's shining platinum fur, and she too greeted them by their new title. "Dreamsavers, the Rememberer regrets that he could not meet you himself," she told them, "but he would like both of you to join him and his counselors at your earliest convenience."

"How about now?" Jenny asked eagerly.

"Fine." Nakeesha was much more agreeable than she had been before, and Jenny knew that Atta Girl's color transformation was one reason for this. It had been Atta's color that Tuhlla had somehow tuned into, to track them wherever they went. This had endangered the underground nation, and the Prime Minister took seriously her duty to help Behrrn protect the people of Chrystellea.

Morgan the Wohtt and Behrrn the Rememberer had realized that the earthlings were a threat to the Chrystelleans too. But they were even more aware that the three earthlings could not remain on their own on the planet's surface for any amount of time and be safe from the Ghanglers.

Without further chatting, Nakeesha led the way through the welcoming crowd and on through the city, toward the castle that rose in the center of the biggest island. Jenny wondered if they would meet Behrrn again in the fun circus room where they'd met before. She didn't ask, though. She knew she'd find out soon and that the prime minister didn't chat unnecessarily.

When they reached the castle, they went in through a different entrance than before. Jenny wondered whether the circus room still existed, since the castle was constructed of dreams, and the Chrystellean people were always dreaming new and different dreams for it.

They went down a long hallway. There were four doors on the left and three on the right. They walked past the three doors on the right. No, now there were four doors on the right and only three doors on the left, until they came to the last door, which was the fourth door on the right. No, now it was on the left again! Jenny was getting a bit dizzy with the changes, but Nakeesha walked over to the blank wall on the right and touched it. Immediately it melted into an entrance to a rock-walled tunnel. She led Jenny and Atta Girl through it, as the wall closed silently behind them.

Inside, the light was dim, and the tunnel wound around and around and even up and down. Erupting from the walls here and there were skeletal hands, or heads, or even whole skeletons that seemed to be almost upon them. Nakeesha was unfazed, but when Jenny overheard her mutter something about "blasted boys," she wondered what "boys" had to do with the tunnel. The skeleton parts didn't look like boys to her. They were definitely man-sized.

They had to duck once to go under a row of boney feet. They dangled from the ceiling of the tunnel, like fishermen lined up on a bridge over a river on a good fishing day.

Finally, the tunnel ended in another rock wall with two skeleton arms raised in a halt position. In a manner-of-fact way, Nakeesha firmly grasped one of the arms, which turned out to be a door handle.

The door opened into an enormous cave room. In the middle of it, Behrrn, Ildirmyrth and several other men and women were gathered around a broad tree stump that had apparently grown through the rock floor. A map was spread out on top of it.

The Rememberer turned toward them with a wide smile and hurried to meet them. His eyes smiled too, as he took in Atta's silvery white fur. Jennifer was glad to see that he hadn't seemed to age while they were on Earth, and she realized that Nitty hadn't, either. At that rate, maybe she'd catch up to Behrrn, and then … she blushed, realizing that she still had a horrendous crush on him, so she quickly turned her thoughts to more practical issues.

She was puzzled by the ocean smell in the room and the sound of ocean water breaking over rocks. She snuck a look around as Ildirmyrth the Masterworker came over to hug her and to pick up Atta, stroking the cat gently, careful not to rub off any of her silvery disguise.

Behrrn introduced them to the others around the tree stump. Jenny responded with smiles, and Atta Girl purred courteously, but then Jenny's gaze wandered again about the cave room. One wall of it was a sculpted-stone bas relief of a wharf and pier, with the ocean behind it and a pirate ship docked there. In the foreground, on the stone dock, was what appeared to be a stone pirate captain wearing an eye patch and smoking a long, curly pipe. Next to that figure, also in stone, was a large pirate chest, with jewels and jewelry spilling out of it on all sides. The pirate figure was facing sideways, looking out to sea. Jenny almost smelled the pipe smoke, and when she looked more carefully, smoke seemed to be coming from it. Its scent, along with the ocean smells, pleasantly filled the room.

In the very center of the room was a tall, *tall*, silvery tree, and in its branches was a house. *A tree house!* The ceiling of the cave was so high that wispy clouds drifted around it. It was the most marvelous place imaginable, although Jenny still wasn't quite comfortable about heights.

Since she had been forced to face up to her fears during the last visit to the White World, though, she had pretty much overcome them; the railing on the stairsteps had put them to rest. Now tree houses, like the one in her friend Willa's backyard, were among her favorite places.

"We're assigning teams to search for the children," Behrrn told Jenny and Atta, after he had greeted them warmly.

"And for Morgan," Jennifer added. "And the Chrystal Gate."

"Morgan?" Behrrn frowned anxiously, and a worried muttering began in the group behind him. "Morgan is gone? And what gate? Can a gate disappear?"

Apparently, Nitty hadn't had time to contact them about *all* that were gone.

"Well," Jenny explained, "when Atta and I arrived in Nitty's cave, we heard Morgan coming." She went on to explain that she and Atta had actually seen the Ghanglers Wohtt-nap Morgan. She told Behrrn how Nitty, when she returned home, had also discovered that the Chrystal Gate was missing—the gate that had brought them here and was *supposed* to take them home again when their visit was over.

"But now …" Although Jenny didn't finish the sentence, Behrrn understood.

"What terrible happenings these are," Behrrn said to them all. "We must let the other searchers know about *these* who are gone, also."

"Avast there, me hearties! Ye're all fergettin' somethin'."

Jennifer looked around, startled to see where this new voice had come from. The stone pirate was now facing the group who'd been studying the map. Jenny shook her head to clear it. She couldn't help wondering if she was hallucinating.

But Behrrn simply turned and calmly spoke to the stone figure. "What is it that we're forgetting, Captain Bahrnee?"

"Why, the high seas a'course. Ye've got nobody searching th' seas."

"That's true, Captain. But of course the Ghanglers have never been known to go to sea, even for short pleasure cruises."

The pirate took the curly pipe out of his mouth to speak. "True enuff, Matey," he admitted. "But I di'nt hear nobody say 'at they'd actual *seen*

Ghanglers take the kiddies. Somebody needs t' be lookin' land 'n' sea fer them kiddies, don't they?"

"They do, indeed, Captain. Can we count on you and your crew to take care of that assignment?"

"Rightee! Now, I'd best start right away t' gather up my crew. First, I'll need t' pervide some 'wages' fer the young rascals afore we set out." He went over to the treasure chest and opened the lid. The jewels, which had appeared to flow out of the chest and onto the dock, simply pulled up with the lid, without losing their scattered shape. Jenny giggled to herself. That fabulous fortune was merely a decorative part of the lid. Captain Bahrnee began to load his huge pockets and arms with the chest's contents. What he pulled out and stowed in his many pockets were things like odd-looking flying machines, slinkies, kites, marbles, water guns, and some things that were like, but not exactly like, Lincoln Logs or Legos. Then he turned to the side again, walked to the end of the wall, and passed through it at the corner.

Behrrn turned back to the others and grinned. "Our Chrystellean boys dream great dreams. But who knows? They might actually find something."

After quiet chuckles, two of the group hastily left the room to spread the word about the missing Wohtt and the missing—immensely valuable—chrystal.

Behrrn continued with the meeting. "Let's see, the Newfangler is already searching this district." He outlined an area on the map. "The Bucklebeams will cover this part, (another area) and you, Ildirmyrth, with your apprentice, will search near here in the Bluhgg Woods area, if that's agreeable."

Jenny looked back at the sculptured wall, and saw that the pirate ship had soundlessly set out to sea.

"Of course," Ildirmyrth concurred. "With your agreement, I shall locate my apprentice now, and we will begin immediately to prepare for our journey. We'll start out through the caves within the hour. We can rest at the top, in the outermost cave, so that we may enter Bluhgg Woods as soon as the starstorms cease."

"Fine." Behrrn assigned another area to a man and woman who also left the conference to get ready, but before he could mark out another, Jennifer interrupted. "I want to help too, Behrrn. I *need* to help! Atta Girl has a disguise now, and so do I." She held up the bags Nitty had given them. "And those poor children and Morgan—maybe we can really help find them. Besides, Nitty says the Chrystal Gate is my only way home now. *Everyone* possible needs to be searching for all the gone, and that includes me!"

"You are right as usual, Jennifer Arthur. Perhaps you could be partnered with Mahlee Kahdel, who will be arriving early in the morning. She knows the Wandering Waters area better than anyone else, so that would be a good designation for you and for Atta Girl, if she cares to go. Meanwhile, you should rest to prepare yourself." He turned to one of the women in the group, "Lehna, would you take them to their sleeping quarters?"

"Wait," Jenny said impulsively. "If it's okay, Behrrn, may we sleep up there?" She pointed hopefully to the tree house.

"That's a perfect idea," Behrrn said. "The Chrystellean boys who dreamed this tree house up made it extremely comfortable for sleepovers." He rolled up the map, and tapped the trunk of the tree-house tree. A rope ladder dropped down.

Jennifer thanked him, as always dazzled by his warm, wonderful smile and his marvelous silver eyes. Behrrn asked a young woman in the group if she would have time to bring food, water, and anything else she could think of that Jennifer and Atta might need. The woman quickly agreed with a smile and hurried off.

Jennifer picked up Atta and started up the ladder, holding on very tightly to both cat and ladder, as the others quietly left the room.

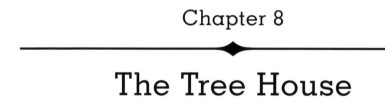

Chapter 8

The Tree House

As tired as she was, Jenny couldn't resist exploring the inside of the tree house. The first thing she noticed was that it was much larger than seemed possible from the outside. There were several doors leading, she supposed, to other rooms.

A large spyglass was aimed out a round window, and was focused over the stone ocean. Jenny looked through it. The night mists were gathering, without the storming stars that plagued that world's surface. She could see dimly through the lenses. She was about to turn away, when she noticed a small island near the horizon. Something was moving on it. Then mist overwhelmed the sight, and Jenny decided to check it out again in the morning.

Metal windup toys and metallic toy banks, pull-string wooden toys, model trains and trucks, and inches-tall action figures all sat on various tables and shelves. Hanging from the ceiling were fabulous flying objects; small planes and balloon-type models mingled with alien bird toys, kites, and small white clouds. She looked at them one at a time, and the one she looked at longest began to fly. It flew as long as her eyes followed it, or until it collided with another of the objects. She figured that the boys had great air battles with them, with each boy "following" a different flying model.

There were shelves stuffed with books too. All of them had the pearly paper pages and silver writing that she remembered were used on the White World. There were games of all kinds too, and although she was pretty sure they *were* games, they weren't quite like anything she'd ever seen. Some seemed to be building sets of some sort.

Through another door was a large closet filled with pillows and huge, fluffy mattresses. She dragged and carried what she needed into the main room, then chose an interesting looking book off a shelf.

Jenny was preparing for sleep when the young woman arrived with a tasty supper and a jug of water for her. She also brought a cotton nightgown with deep lace trimming. Even the lace was as soft as silk and the gown was lush to sleep in, especially considering that she usually slept in one of her dad's old T-shirts.

Is there anything else you may need, Dreamsaver?" The woman asked in her soft voice.

"I can't think of a thing," Jennifer sighed contentedly, while looking around her. "Except, is there any kind of reading light here, preferably one I can turn off without getting out of bed?"

"Indeed." She pulled a small tree out of the corner—a *real* tree, with peculiar fruits growing on it, all different and each as clear as glass. Perched on one branch was a large bird, something like a parrot but not exactly. "Light please, Marvin," the woman requested. The bird plucked a lantern from a branch. It was like a ship's lantern but smaller, and it lit as it was lifted. He perched on the headboard of the bed, and the light gleamed right over her shoulder through the night mists right where she wanted it. Jenny thanked her as she left and snuggled into bed with the book she'd chosen. She was sleepier than she realized, though, so she soon put the book aside and said, "Light off please, Marvin." The bird croaked, "Yo, Missy, I hen't finished that page yet."

Startled, Jenny looked up at the bird. Lots of parrots could talk of course, but apparently this one could read too. She grinned and opened the book again to the page she'd been reading. She waited for a few minutes to let him finish. "Sleep tight, Missy," Marvin said. Then he put the light back on the branch where, with a gentle shhhhh, it turned off. Marvin tucked his head under a wing and apparently was asleep already.

In the morning, when the night mists had cleared, Jenny checked out the view through the spyglass again. The view was clear, and there was definitely a small island out there, but she saw nothing moving on it. She decided she had seen a movement of the mists.

She rebrushed Atta Girl's fur to a gleaming white and dressed herself in the clothes Nitty had given her. The clothes felt strange, with the long skirt and petticoats brushing softly against her legs. She said goodbye and thank you to Marvin and picked up the cloak, her bag, and Atta Girl. Thinking about the trip ahead, on the surface, she scrambled down the rope ladder without thinking about how high aboveground she was starting from. At the bottom, someone had set a lovely breakfast on the huge tree stump where the map had been spread out the evening before. A note was there too, inviting Jenny and Atta to enjoy their meals. Atta Girl looked around and saw a bowl on the ground, chock-full of something with a luscious, fresh-fish smell. She began immediately to devour its contents. Jenny looked around her as she sat down to enjoy her own meal and noticed that Captain Bahrnee wasn't back, although the pirate ship was docked again.

Behrrn came into the cave room with a squarish little woman. Actually, she was more like a cube than a square; about three feet high, wide, and deep, whichever way one looked, and her serviceable clothes seemed to turn corners around her.

"Hmph," the woman snorted. "I'm just exactly the height I should oughta be, and my other dimensions are as absolutely perfect as that one."

Jenny was startled, because what she'd just been thinking was that the strange little woman was so very short—in all directions.

"Of course you are, ma'am," she said hurriedly. "You are definitely a very fine shape."

The woman hmphed again, thinking that Jennifer was a tall, skinny thing and probably wouldn't be much help in the search.

"Jennifer Arthur and Atta Girl, this is Mahlee Kahdel," Behrrn said quickly. "She'll be your guide through the Wandering Waters. Miz

Kahdel, these are two of the three famous Dreamsavers, Jennifer Arthur and Atta Girl."

"Hmmmm. Well, I reckon th' two of you did us all a right smart favor, savin' the Dream of Color fer us all. And I reckon you hen't really skinny at all. You and th' cat must be just about perfect fer the kind you are, whatever kind that is."

Jenny smiled down at the tiny woman. "The kind we both are is earthlings," she told her. "I'm an earthling girl, and Atta Girl is an earthling cat."

"Ha! If yer the girl, and that there's the cat, how's to come *her* name be Atta *Girl*, an' *yours* be Jennifer. I reckon ye be trying to noodlewink me, aren't ye?"

"No, I …"

"Whoa! What happy surprise is this?" Behrrn's sudden exclamation saved Jenny from trying to explain. Instead she, Atta, and Mahlee all followed the Rememberer's look. Captain Bahrnee was now back in his place, standing sideways and looking out to sea. Standing near him was a very real boy, about eight years old. He clutched a stick that was tied to a bundle that slumped on the floor. He wore a floppy, wide-brimmed hat with an ivy-like vine growing out of the hat band, and his eyes were focused intently on the table full of food.

With a slow, crunching sound, the captain turned toward the room and took the pipe from his mouth.

"Ahoy, mates! Me ship, me crew, an' me found this young 'un on th' deserted isle out yonder." He crunched again, as he waved his free hand out to the granite sea. "He were in a bad way, fer there he'nt no food er water whatsumnever out thar. I told ye we should be searchin' the seas …"

"You did indeed, Captain. And where is that fine crew of yours, now?"

While they talked, Jenny signaled to the boy to come to the table and eat. He came eagerly, although he ducked his head shyly.

"Me crew?" The captain took a deep puff on his pipe, filling the cave with its scent. "Why, they's at home with their mams and pops, they be. Wouldn't want their folks worryin', what with all them other young 'uns missin' here and on the surface."

Behrrn thanked him as Jennifer heaped food from her plate onto a plate for the boy. He picked up a fork and dug into it eagerly. Captain Bahrnee turned stiffly to settle back into his profile pose.

Behrrn waited until the boy had satisfied himself and finished the water Jenny had poured for him. As he waited, he chatted quietly with Mahlee and Jenny about their search plans.

Finally the boy sat back in his stool and burped loudly, quickly excusing himself.

"Well, lad, my name is Behrrn. And besides being a valiant adventurer, who are you?"

The boy looked up at Behrrn hesitantly before he answered. "My name be Hahrell, but folks all call me Rell," he said, "and I be from Boggsburgh. I was right hungered and thirsted just now. Thanks be fer yer hospitality."

"I'm sure you were hungry. How long were you on the island, and how did you come to be there?"

"I were there through two starstorms, sir," he answered. "I sheltered under a overhang them times, and daytimes I looked for food and water, but I didn't find none. I looked for something to fix me raft with too, but I didn't find anything for that neither."

"A raft? That must have been fun. How did you come to be on a raft?" Behrrn's questions were easygoing, and Rell gained confidence as he spoke.

"I done built it, but it do seem I di'nt built it too good."

"And then, of course, you needed to try it out. Right?"

"Right, sir, I just wanted a leetle bit of an adventure, y'know."

"And it turned out to be a bit more than you bargained for. Well, Rell, we'll get word to your parents that you're fine, and that you'll be home, soon." Turning to the others, Behrrn said, "Boggsburgh lies just beyond the Wandering Waters. If it's agreeable with the three of you, perhaps he could go there with you?"

"Acourse!" Mahlee answered, smiling. Her smile stretched around the corners of her head, bent the straight lines that bracketed her mouth into gentle curves, and crinkled her eyes reassuringly.

"Wandering Waters?" Rell's eyes went wide with the question. "Ben't nobody except Swamp Tribers what knows the way outta there! And there be monsters! Invisible monsters! Hen't nobody but them Tribers what kin go in and come out again."

"As for monsters, there are indeed dangerous creatures in the Wandering Waters, but unless you enter the waters, you are safe from them." Behrrn grinned. "I don't believe there are any "NO SWIMMING" signs posted there, but don't swim anyway and you should be quite safe."

"But they got some things called Invisible Ones and ..."

"The so-called invisible ones haven't threatened the area for hundreds and hundreds of galaxy turns. Our wisest scientists have determined that a dimension that wasn't intended for our planet was somehow caught and folded into our planet underneath the Wandering Waters when both it and our world were just coming into creation. The people of the Waters District, since earliest remembered time, have referred to that threat as 'The Dread'. The theory is that it no longer has access to our surface, probably because time has drawn more dust and dirt into our orbit and settled here, deepening our surface."

"But ..." Rell sputtered.

"Because of that, our wisest people called the phenomenon 'The Dread Dimension.' But that is ancient history, not a current threat."

Anyway, Ms. Kahdel is kin to the Water Tribers, Rell, and she comes and goes frequently. You couldn't have a better guide, and the swamp monsters stay clear of frequently used trails. The quickest way to your home and family is through that area, Hahrell, but you've no need to fear, as long as all of you stay with her and out of the waters."

"We'll all watch out for ye," Mahlee assured the boy, but Jennifer wondered what help she and Atta Girl would be for finding their way and fighting monsters, not to mention finding Morgan, the Gate Chrystal, and those poor stolen children.

The young woman who had helped them the previous night bustled in at that point with a pair of shoes like most White Worlders seemed to wear. "I noticed your shoes," she told Jenny breathlessly, "and realized that they would give away your differentness to Ghanglers right away.

I found these. I hope they fit, but if they don't we'll find some that do, *before* you join the search on the surface."

"Thank you for your alertness," Behrrn said quickly. "I should have thought of that too."

"Me too," Jenny added as she tried on the shoes. She realized that her Adidas would have blown her cover right away. "These fit just super!" The shoes looked like puffy white suede pouches. Pleats in the material flexed around her ankles, and the shoes and lining were marshmallow soft. She hoped they were sturdy enough for the search, but she knew it was what nearly all the women and girls here wore, so they must be fairly tough.

"Thank you," she said. "Now I'm ready for anything." *Almost anything,* she added to herself, still wondering what might face them in Wandering Waters Territory.

Chapter 9

—————————◆—————————

Tunneling

Now that they were on their way, Rell couldn't believe his luck. "I got meself stranded on a desert island, got rescued by a bunch of boys and a Pirate Captain in a Pirate Ship—and now, I've up an' met the Rememberer hisself and two of the Dreamsavers, Jennifer Arthur and Atta Girl, the Dreamsaver cat, in person. And Jenny is purty, too!" He shook himself with excitement. "She and Atta Girl will be going through Wandering Waters with Ms. Kahdel and me, but I ain't sure what's happened to that cat." After all the stories he'd heard about her color, Atta was as white as everything else, except he'd noticed her eyes were a most amazing color! "Yellow," he thought, remembering what he'd been taught about the names of colors he'd felt in public masterworks. "*Real* yellow!"

And the best part was that they'd be going right through Wandering Waters, and Behrrn said it was "safe as butterin' toast" with Ms. Kahdel along. When he got home he'd be a hero himself. *There weren't nobody in Boggsburgh what ever went into that place, not t' mention coming out safe again! A'course I aren't tiptotally certain about that part, but Ms. Kahdel seemed to know what she were about, and the Rememberer wouldn't send us all in there with 'er if it were as bad as folks said, would he?*

As they went on, Jenny was more and more grateful for the pouch-like shoes. When they entered Wandering Waters Territory they seemed almost to float over the rough, rocky pathways. The area made her think of the Louisiana bayous, where her family had gone to visit Mom's best friend from college. But the whiteness of the trees and mosses, and even the nearly transparent ground with its lacy worm tunnels, made this part of the White World a kind of fairyland, with liquid-silver rivers running through and porcelain-white trees growing out of that silvery water. The humidity was as bad or worse than in Bluhgg Woods, though. The paths coiled like snakes through it, but Mahlee proceeded confidently, as if she traveled this way every day of her life. She pulled what Jenny thought of as an upside-down sled. It was strapped to her shoulders, and the lower side, with a large bundle tied to it. It had bouncy tires, too, that seemed to roll along merrily, without tiring her.

Rell was plenty glad to be out of the dripping-wet caverns of Bluhgg Woods, anyway. Jenny said she and Willa had renamed it "Ugh Woods" when they were there before, and they'd had it about right. It were a slimy place, with trees reaching out to grab and itty bitty snakes slithering here and there. Sweat ran down his neck, making him feel even hotter than a thermometer could show. While he was there, he felt as if he was melting, right down to his bones.

He readjusted the straps on his pack as they entered Wandering Waters Territory, and thought how glad he was that Jennifer had shown him how to fix it like she fixed hers. She called 'em "backpacks," and it were right handy to have his hands free, just in case.

Jenny and Rell chatted about the scenery and about their lives. Rell was super interested in Jennifer's stories about her younger brother, Warren, and their amazing world, chock-full of colors—*real* colors, not just memories of Behrrn's dreams. He told Jenny about how much he'd like to meet Warren.

She had to admit to him that meeting Warren probably wouldn't be possible. "As a matter of fact," she admitted, after clearing a sudden lump in her throat, "right now, I'm not at all sure that I'll ever see him again. That's one reason why we're trying to find the other chrystal for the Chrystal Gate, as well as Morgan the Wohtt and *all* the lost children. But I have no idea where to look for that chrystal, or even what it looks like."

Rell was silent for a long while, saddened by Jenny's problem. Then, when they were well into the Wandering Waters, he decided to take an optimistic approach. "Be sure to tell Warren about that there funny-lookin' island," he said as they approached a small dollop of land in the waters. It had what appeared to be a perfectly round tunnel through it, with light showing from the other side. Jenny looked back when they'd passed it, though, and there was no opening to be seen on the other side.

"And over there is a leaper bug. It spits, but the spit don't hurt; it just be sticky."

"We have spitting bugs on Earth too," Jenny told him. We call them grasshoppers, and the sticky juice they spit is brown. That's why we call it 'tobacco juice.' But ours are nowhere near as big as that one is." The bug Rell had pointed out was the size of a half-grown Labrador retriever. Jenny edged away, hopefully out of spitting distance.

"Stormin' stars! Leaper bugs clear on another planet? Wowee!"

Jenny and Rell walked along drowsily behind Mahlee Kahdell for a bit.

Rell was thinking about all the other worlds and the creatures and colors on them. Atta Girl explored along the path's sides, carefully staying out of the waters that flowed alongside.

Jenny was thinking about home. She wiped sweat from her forehead with her sleeve and remembered a visit she and her family made to Louisiana one summer when they rode in a canoe through the bayous. The Wandering Waters even smelled boggy like those did. The bayous were beautiful, and so were the Waters, but what if this water was also home to alligators, like the Louisiana bayous were? She pushed back a worry that if the invisible Dread Dimension hadn't been around for centuries, what if this were about the time for it to return?

Rell interrupted her thoughts, pointing. "And them there be sportball trees "Be sure to tell Warren that whatever ball game he'd want to play, they'd grow it for him. Just if he'd make up a rhyme about the game, then in a minute or two he could pluck the right ball fer it right off. And look over there, them are—"

"What in the White!" Mahlee Kahdell's sudden exclamation stopped Rell, Jenny, and Atta Girl in their tracks. With their guide in the lead, they were facing a spidery network of pathways in all directions. "These should not be here." She looked around at all the paths, frowning with confusion. "I must have taken a wrong turn somewhere, but I can't imagine where. We'll have to retrace our path to find where I went wrong, and quickly. We don't want to get caught out here when the starstorms come."

Jennifer looked around too, trying to count the paths ahead of them, but they seemed to change in shape and number no matter how carefully she counted them.

Mahlee turned right around and started back the way they'd come. The others followed her quickly. Jenny remembered the White World's nightly starstorms all too well.

As they hurried back, Rell was not as talkative as he had been, but Atta Girl was sending Jenny frequent mind messages. *There isss something larrrrge in the water. Ssstay ffaar fffrom it.* She scratched her way up into the chalk-white trees again and reported, *There are water crrreaturessss with large teeth and clawssss watching usssss. Bewarrrre!*

Jennifer hurried her steps even more, placing her feet carefully in the center of the path they were following, although she had no idea where they were heading. She was beginning to worry that their guide was as confused as she was. Bone-white scraggle-branches clawed at them, huge lizards slithered across their path, and menacing sounds came from the waters all around them.

Rell picked up a stout white stick about as long as he was tall. "Don't be feared, Jennifer. Since Warren be not here, I'll take keer of you and Atta and Miz Kahdel too." He swung his stick around as if it were a sword and then walked on, using it like a walking stick.

Abruptly, there were tangled paths again, uncountable pathways leading away in all directions. Jenny and Rell looked at Mahlee hopefully but were not reassured.

Atta Girl dropped from the trees and headed down one of the paths. *I hear voicesss down thissss way. Other wayssss are only thick misssstsss.*

Rell and Jennifer looked at each other; Mahlee Kahdel started after Atta, and the others followed. Nothing else happened to show them a better way.

Rell gave his walking stick to Jenny and found another for Mahlee Kahdel. Finally, he selected and prepared one for himself, feeling that he'd done the best he could to prepare them all for whatever came next. The path that Atta led them down seemed as threatening as the rest, but they all knew that if they kept changing paths, they would get absolutely nowhere, and Atta Girl assured them that there really were people ahead—way ahead.

They proceeded cautiously, though, because they didn't know *who* those people might be.

Suddenly a flock of small, harmless-looking birds attacked them viciously with beaks and claws; the travelers ran frantically ahead to escape them.

When their path entered a long tunnel, the swamps deepened and joined a small river that ran alongside them. When they lost the attacking birds they slowed to a careful walk again. They shushed each other, listened to the echoing silence, and stared through the milky mists that drifted even there. There were small, hushed noises sometimes interrupting the silence, but the sounds seemed as confused as they were. The mist cleared for the moment, and they saw a giraffe pacing in confused circles. It looked to Jennifer like those she'd seen at the zoo, only it was just about the size of Atta Girl except for its very long neck. Atta interrupted one of its frantic circles and stood nose to nose with it for a moment. *He issss lossst,* she reported back to her companions. *I have suggested that he come with ussss.*

They moved along carefully, calling to one another to keep themselves aimed ahead and not going in circles. The giraffe quietly moved after them, its long neck bobbing gently.

Their progress was slow, but they walked closely together, hoping against hope to reach the tunnel's end *soon.* It coiled around in all directions, even up and down, but at least on this path, there was only one pathway. However, not only was the tunnel confusing, but it *felt* confused, as well. It looked like a natural cave-tunnel, but its stalactites and stalagmites grew out of the tunnel's sides instead of from the floor and ceiling.

Jenny was more and more grateful for the shoe pouches that she'd been given, because the floor of the tunnel was rocky and some of the rocks were sharp. Even the sharpest ones didn't hurt her feet through the shoes, but she avoided them as much as possible. She needed the shoes to last.

She focused on her steps, one after the other, while reaching out to her companions with her voice when the mists veiled them. Atta Girl stayed close and rubbed against her ankles, making small, anxious mewing sounds.

"Groaaarrr!" A tremendous roar shattered the silence of the tunnel, and at the same time, Rell hollered, "Snake!"

Jenny had no idea whether the enormous snake that had dropped in front of her was what had roared or whether it was poisonous. All she knew for sure was that its long, flicking tongue was poised to strike, right at her face.

A thick cloud of mist swept suddenly between her and the snake, and while she was shielded from it she stepped quickly to one side and raised her walking stick. At that moment the snake's head, with its darting, forked tongue, shot through the mist at the spot where she had just been standing. She swung the heavy stick, hitting it on its head, and at that very same moment a tiny white lion leaped out of the mists to attack the tail end of it, snarling and biting. Dazed and frightened, the enormous snake shrank to the ground and twisted its way into hiding.

While it was still confused, the travelers broke into a run to get through the tunnel before any more monster-types showed up. The mists, however, got thicker and thicker as they ran downhill.

Jenny reached for Atta Girl, but she wasn't at her side as usual. She was running along next to the small white lion.

The tunnel leveled out and began to rise again. Running was harder, but the thought of more hidden threats in the white-out mists kept them going. Jenny's breath was coming in sharp gasps, but Atta Girl and the lion were moving along easily, while the voices of Mahlee and Rell were staying ahead of her. The tunnel echoed with the sounds of their running and sounds of slithering, fluttering, crawling, and skittering things echoed too.

"Stormin' Stars!" Mahlee called out as she tripped over a rough spot on the floor. Then, as she righted herself she quickly assured them, "I'm all right, dears." She went on. She was a little slower, a little lamer, but she was still going. The mists thinned as the tunnel climbed higher. Jenny slowed too, to stay with Mahlee and Rell, and then, when she also stumbled a bit with fatigue, she felt Atta Girl rub against her leg as if to reassure herself that Jenny was alright, before she returned to her new friend. They both stayed near her then, as they all plodded on.

The group clambered upward until they suddenly bumped into one another, like traffic sometimes does, when a car in front stops suddenly and unexpectedly. Mahlee the guide had stopped first, when she came up short at the end of the floor of the tunnel.

Oh, the tunnel went on all right, but there was no more path—only the fearful waters that continued to flow through it.

Mahlee stuck the walking stick Rell had made for her into the water, but it didn't reach the bottom. It was definitely too deep for wading, even if they could deal with whatever creatures lived in it. She leaned against a relatively smooth section of wall, and took deep breaths to calm herself. Atta Girl abandoned her new friend again to come and thread herself around Jenny's legs.

"If on'y I had my raft, still,' Rell said. "But I'd hafta shore 'er up somewhat to make it a bit hardier."

There was a pause as the others tried to come up with something more practical than retreating, back the way they'd come. Finally, Jenny's gaze settled on Mahlee's upside-down sled.

"If we could turn that thing over and somehow waterproof it, it just might work as a raft," she suggested. "But …" She looked all around the tunnel but came up with no answers. "But there's nothing here to use for that. Too bad, Because even if Mahlee Kahdell's carrier thing is long and heavy, it it was watertight, it'd float just fine."

Mahlee Kahdel looked doubtful, but Rell began walking about looking for the biggest, most solid sideways stalactites. He chose one and swung on it until it cracked at its wide base. Then Jenny helped him to pull it free. "Okay, it's worth a try," she said. "If Mahlee is willing, I can tear strips from some of these petticoats I'm wearing to lash the pieces together and then build up the sled-raft's sides."

"These here hen't be so heavy as they look," Rell agreed, after Mahlee had nodded in tired agreement. "But how kin we make it leak proof, even if we could built it? There hen't be nothing in this here tunnel to use."

"Hmmm," Mahlee shook herself upright and looked thoughtful for a bit, then pulled her wheeled baggage around in front of her. "Maybe there *is* something we could use." She spread out her bundle, and chose the largest package in it to open as she explained; "whenever I come to visit my Water Tribe friends and family, I bring them things that they can't get here. This time—she triumphantly pulled out and held up a fat white candle, and what turned out to be sort of like a high tech lighter. "This time it was candles that I brought. I've got dozens of 'em."

Chapter 10

The Raft

Mahlee Kahdel leaned on a ledge and thought and thought and thought about how she could have become lost in the Waters. The paths through it were as familiar to her as her own backyard. Or at least they always were *before*. What could have happened here? Where had she gone wrong?

She squeezed her eyes shut, as if that might help her concentrate, but eyelids couldn't close out her awareness of her fellow travelers looking at her hopefully, waiting for her to come up with a solution. She reopened her eyes. One thing that would help right at the moment was in another one of her bundles ... it was a picnic dinner, and she knew for sure that dinner could be a huge boost to morale, and *might* even give them helpful ideas. She spread out chockets and dumplings, kept warm in a huge wide-mouthed crock. There was frinnberry juice, whellyflour biscuits, and yummy tunket tarts too. The hungry group dug in eagerly, while Atta and the lion went foraging for food better suited to their taste.

As they ate, Mahlee got herself busy dripping wax freehand into what they hoped would be the bottom of their raft. Jenny and Rell did the same, using some matches that Rell pulled out of his pocket. When he'd taken his raft along, he'd figured they might come in handy someday. Soon they turned the raft over to its topside, and began sealing openings there and on its sides.

Jennifer believed the fragrance of candle wax would always remind her of this welcome feast-in-a-tunnel. Her grandmother used to say, "Hunger is the best sauce." They were all hungry, but the food was tasty even without that special sauce. She wondered, though, if the waterway ahead would lead them *out* of the tunneled river to another end of their path or only take them deeper into danger.

The out-slanted sides were becoming well sealed, and they all had hopes that the cool water would keep the wax cool enough to last. Finally the whole thing was sealed, and all the bundles were tied (with one of Jennifer's petticoats, torn into strips) to a smaller trailer raft made of more lashed-together stalactites, which they tied to the larger raft. Before they tied themselves to the large raft, they covered the bundles and backpacks with a waterproof tarp from Mahlee's assortment of supplies.

To Jenny's eyes, the whole thing looked pretty rickety, but it was the best they could do. The tunnel waters were smooth as glass as far as they could see, although that was only to where the cave curved again.

They all piled onto the upside-down sled-raft, and "safety-belted" themselves onto it with rag strips, even Atta Girl and the small lion. The giraffe skittered back on the dry tunnel ledge and refused to board, so they reluctantly pushed themselves into the water without it, using all the poles Rell had prepared. They looked ahead nervously, and after an "S" turn or two they finally did hear voices bouncing off the rocky walls ahead. There was no way to tell how far ahead the people were, but they knew they hadn't passed any on the way, so they *must* be somewhere nearby. Okay, so that way of thinking didn't prove anything, but it perked them up a bit. They poled and drifted gently on, hope looking for hope.

Even though the water was smooth it wasn't friendly, as Behrrn had warned them. He'd only said not to go *in* the Waters, though. He hadn't said anything about going *on* them. Weird sharklike fish leaped across the raft from time to time, more than one skimming near enough to the travelers to bring hearts into throats, and once a leaping fish with sharp ventral fins sliced a shallow cut across Jenny's hand. Atta Girl and the lion leaped for that creature, but, like all of them, they'd been lashed to the raft so they couldn't be swept off. The water creature dove in on the other side of the raft and swam away.

"Bats!" Jenny squealed later, throwing her arms over her head to protect it. *Some* kind of flying things flocked toward them from above, but they swarmed near the ceiling of the underground tunnel and over the raft in the direction from which the travelers had come, as if they hadn't even noticed the raft and its passengers. They clattered and squeaked and their wings flapped with sounds like slapping leather. Jenny thought they resembled small dragons more than bats. Although their bodies were only the size of small dogs, their wingspans were wider than Dad's desk back home, and their long, glittering teeth and claws looked like they meant business. But if they weren't interested in the raft riders, what might they be flying from … or *to?*

Then for a while it was peaceful, drifting with the current, if you could ignore the eerie underwater shapes nosing near and often bumping the raft. The travelers were all tired from walking, so they leaned back against each other and took long, deep breaths.

Jenny's thoughts flicked through memories of home. These thoughts were almost, but not quite, enough to make her forget where she actually was. She thought about her family and wondered whether it was night or day on Earth, in the USA, in Northern California, on Miller Street. "There is no distance too great for love or for prayer," Mom used to say. *But what about distances across universes?* Jenny's eyes threatened tears, but she refocused on the job at hand.

They heard a different sound in the distance ahead of them, but they only got worried when it grew louder and louder. "Rapids," Jenny whispered at the same time that Mahlee shouted, "Rapids ahead!" They all tried to pole themselves backward, but the current was strong and getting stronger. When the sound became a thunder-rage, they sighted the top of a craggy rock ahead to their right. "Steer to the left," Mahlee directed, "away from the rock. With any luck, it'll just be a little rock, and the drop ahead a small one." But as they came up on that watery horizon, they saw that neither the drop nor the rock were small.

The raft rocked crazily, and they were poling both walls to keep from being tossed into the stalactites or into the deep, churning whirlpool that swept around the jagged rock.

Mahlee directed Rell to keep trying to push the raft away from the sides of the tunnel, as she and Jenny focused with all their might to keep the raft *out* of the whirlpool, *away* from that jagged rock. But it was no use. The whirlpool sucked them deeper and deeper, up against the craggy sides of the rock.

Then, for no reason that they could see, the whirlpool slowed to a stop, and only gentle waves were left, lapping gently at the sides of the raft. A quiet current deposited them into a smooth, underground bay which washed the raft and its occupants into shallows that lapped onto a shore covered with many tossed about, small, rounded pebbles. On the far side of that little shore, with a very short climb up to it, the pathway continued on, once more accompanied by the silver river.

As they waded onto that shore, a feeling came over Jenny. It was as if her mom stood beside her for just a moment, just long enough to smile, and whisper, *See?*

"I do see, Mom," Jennifer whispered back, 'Do you know, Mom, that *you're* a space traveler now, too?"

The pathway aimed even more upward and the small group trudged on, each hoping the way wasn't much higher or much farther.

Soon they could see a round area of a different, smoother white ahead of them. It must be the tunnel's exit. It had to be!

Chapter 11

Tunnel's End

The sweet scent of fresh air seeped into the tunnel, filling them with hope and adrenaline needed to speed them until they reached the very top of the path that was, just as they'd hoped, the *other* end of the tunnel.

But there was a heavy, white iron grille gate over the exit, and the gate didn't open from inside.

The grid was heavy. Solid. Immovable. It was a slide-away design, with the lock way over to one side, completely out of reach from inside. They each tried to move it separately and then all together, but it wouldn't budge.

A few small storming night stars sifted through the grill. Ms. Kahdel took off her heavy cloak and tucked its corners into the crisscrossed metal rods, screening off most of the opening. She led them back, away from the grid to a wide, flat area in the pathway.

"Suppertime and then we sleep," she announced. "The cave and grill at least provide shelter from the starstorms, which have begun for tonight."

They heard voices again and even laughter, and they smelled delicious food smells. They hollered all together, but nobody came. Jennifer sighed. They probably couldn't be heard over the happy noises the people on the other side of the metal grid were making.

She sat on the cave floor, too exhausted and scared to eat the leftovers Mahlee had set out. She readjusted her backpack to sit more Comfortably against the cave wall and took a bite out of a bahroot sandwich, but her thoughts kept circling. *What if nobody ever came? What if they came, but they were Ghanglers or some other bad guys?* She slid farther down on her pack. *What if …?* Sleep stopped her questions, but her dreams didn't bring her any answers.

While Jenny, Mahlee, and Rell slept, Atta and Beauregard, the lion, slipped through the grid and found a camp full of people, where many snores rumbled through the starstorming night. Some campers, rolled up protectively in in thick, quilted blankets, were sleeping outdoors under the storming stars, and some, from the other snores they could hear, dreamed comfortably in tents and trailers. There were even several animals, mostly free-grazing or standing asleep, protected by their own White World furs. A few were in cages, but the cage doors stood open. Atta Girl and Beau hid in the tough shrubbery at first, and Atta was grateful that most of her whiteness was still on her. Beau crouched slightly in front of her, to shield her from view as much as he could. No one but Jennifer had ever before tried to protect her from anything. Atta felt a brand new warmth in the area of her little heart, which was, of course, quite large for a cat. Quickly, she glanced again at Beauregard. He was the most impressive male she'd ever seen.

But the thing to think about now, was getting help for Jennifer and the others in their group.

Admonishing Atta Girl to stay out of sight, since her silver was beginning to wear off, Beauregard slipped through clumps of white grass and shrubs to one of the occupied animal cages. All of the cages were carved with circus themes: clowns, acrobats, high wire artists, tumblers, and other characters. The most remarkable thing about the cages, though, was that the gates weren't just open—they had no locks.

Quietly the small white lion spoke to the enormous three-horned manicunzel, who was already awake and busy nibbling on a large clump of grass that had been tossed into a corner of its cage. "Please, large horned sir," Beauregard asked, "which of the humans in this camp might be most helpful to unexpected newcomers?'

The manticunzel was a beast of few words, and the answer he projected to Beau was gravelly and hard to understand. After a moment or two, though, the lion realized that the manticunzel was telling him, "any one of them."

Mahlee and Rell were still sleeping when Jenny woke up, but Atta and Beau weren't. They weren't even there, and Jenny's stomach churned with panic. *Where were they?*

She sighed with relief when she saw them, even though they were on the *other* side of the grilled gate!

Helllp isss coming, Atta reassured her through the grill. *A big mannn is lookinnng for the key rrrright noooow.*

Chapter 12

The Campground

"Hello, Hello, Hello!" A large, smiling man with an enormous, elaborately curled moustache approached. He was carrying an ornate key that was as big as a binder. He extended his other hand as if to shake hands and then laughingly shook his head at himself. "I guess I'd best open the gate before the handshakes begin."

Matching his actions to his words, he quickly fit the key into the oversized padlock and turned it. The gate pulled open, and he removed the key, grandly sliding back the gate to allow the travelers into the cleared opening. The diameter of that area was about the length of a pro football stadium and circular in shape. Paths led from it in all directions, but, as with the paths at the other crossroads, they couldn't be counted without confusion, and they never seemed to head in the same direction for more than a few moments. There were grill gates over some of them, but since new ones seemed to appear all the time, while others disappeared—grills and all—the smiling man explained that the campers had simply given up on making new ones.

Makeshift tents were erected among elaborate wagons with men, women, and children usually circulating around them. Right then, though, they were all crowded behind the man with the key.

"Welcome to the Society of Stranded Campers. I am Grehssekker the Great Illusionist," he said as he enthusiastically pumped each of the travelers' hands. But he couldn't continue his speech, because the whole group crowded around him, some assuring Jenny and all of welcome, and others asking what had been happening in the last few days outside of Wandering Waters Territory.

As Jenny's group entered the area, Mahlee told the campgrounders they were searching for many mysteriously missing children, and all the parents gave thankful looks at their own little ones who played happily underfoot. She added that Morgan, the Wonderful, Wandering Wohtt, had been kidnapped by the Ghanglers too, and Rell confided that he was trying to get back to his parents in Burkesville.

Jenny didn't mention the missing chrystal. It would be too confusing to explain it, and she was pretty sure these stranded people didn't have it.

Later, after they'd been welcomed by everyone, they were divided among the fortunate families who had arrived there with tents or wagons. Jennifer was invited to settle her belongings with a cheerful family of three. Atta Girl and Beauregard made themselves comfortable underneath that family's wagon. The wagon resembled what Jenny thought of as a gypsy wagon, with an arched roof and windows, but instead of colorful designs all over, there were funny and whimsical carvings everywhere, inside and out. There were Ahnii, the mom; Dohrwen, the dad; and their beautiful two-year-old daughter, Neyahbee, whom they called Little Bee.

At first Little Bee hid shyly behind Ahnii's skirts, but she peeked out and smiled a wonderfully sweet smile at Jennifer, and Jenny smiled back. It was love at first sight!

Dohrwen and Ahnii worked together preparing a tasty breakfast for the four of them, plus something for Atta Girl and Beauregard. Jennifer set the dishes on a tablecloth spread on the floor. Delicious aromas throughout the campsite told of breakfasts being prepared in all the camps. Ahnii said they should hurry, so that Jenny would have time to explore the area and meet everyone before the community lunch, which would be followed by a special Illusion Spectacle that Grehssekker had announced would be held in honor of the newcomers. Soon, the toddler attached herself to Jenny, sitting close beside her on the wagon floor as the family ate breakfast.

Later, with Ahnii's smiling permission, Little Bee hid behind Jenny's skirts as the two of them, with Atta and Beauregard trailing behind, explored the small, circular community.

Emerging from the wagon, they met Mahlee, who'd come to check on Jenny.

Jennifer enthusiastically reassured her that she was more than cozy and asked, "And you, how do you like your hostess?" Mahlee Kahdel grinned clear around the corners of her face.

"Oh, merciful mists!" she exclaimed happily. "My hostess Jhinlillee is one of my Wandering Waters kinfolk, and she's been catching me up on all the news, at least up until a few days ago, when the Dread Dimension came upon the territory. "The Dread" is what these folks call the awful confusion that's taken place here. It's trapped all of them and now us in this central area. They are doing the very best they can with it, though, until they figure a way out again."

Jhinlillee caught up with them and announced breathlessly, "Oh, goodness, Mahlee, my mind must be sliding around like these here pathways, I'm so forgetful! I'll wager you haven't heard that your sister gave birth to twins about two weeks ago! They were early, as twins tend to be, and they were a girl and a boy!"

Mahlee turned to her hostess eagerly, bombarding her with questions. As they chatted, Jenny and Little Bee walked on toward Rell. He was playing ball with another boy about his age. He barely stopped long enough, when they called to him, to tell them that he couldn't be better, having been invited into a home with the family of the boy he was playing with.

Jenny's brain felt dizzy, trying to remember the names and faces of everybody in the stranded community. Mahlee and Jhinlillee were still deep in conversation about Mahlee's sister's new babies.

Lunch was a community affair, with everyone sitting at folding tables grouped in the middle of a huge tent that was erected in the center of the campground. The tables circled an odd, circular picket fence that seemed taller at some times or places, and shorter at others. Inside the fence was a small patch of ground about six feet across, and in the middle of it was a hole in the ground. A sign was posted on the fence that announced, "CAUTION! VERY VERY VERY DEEP HOLE." When lunch was over, the tables were folded and pushed to the sides of the tent. Chairs were rearranged into audience-style rows, with a section of tent wall left clear on one side for Grehssekker to set up his "magic" equipment. As the show began, Jenny and Little Bee found seats in the front row and settled down to watch.

Chapter 13

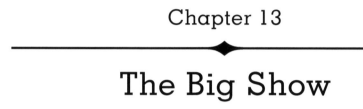

The Big Show

Grehssekker, now recognizable only by his curly moustache, was dressed in clown-like raggedy clothing. He bowed to Mahlee Kahdel, to Jennifer with Little Bee, to Rell, and then to the audience in general. Still silent, he began his act.

At first the tricks reminded Jenny too much of those popular with magicians and illusionists on Earth. She acutely felt the lack of color when always-white scarves were pulled from Grehssekker's sleeves and ears and from Rell's as well.

Her mind wandered back home again. Her brother Warren had a magic kit he practiced with, complete with a top hat. He'd love this show, although Grehssekker wore a kind of derby hat, instead. She always laughed at the corny jokes that went with Warren's banter, and she couldn't help giggling too, when he tried to make his voice sound mysterious. She resolved right then that if she ever got home, she'd *only* laugh at the right places.

She began to pay more attention when Grehssekker's stunts became increasingly unusual. He went through the "disappearing lady" act, but he used a large, friendly dog instead of a lady, and when he brought the dog back, it happily licked the illusionist's face and ears.

It looked like "sawing through a lady" was coming up. Jenny had seen this before on TV, but she could never figure out how it was done.

This person being sawed in half wasn't a glittery-dressed woman as they always were on Earth. Instead, Grehssekker chose a chubby man with a huge nose from the crowd. The box the illusionist ushered him into was barely large enough to contain him. Once the man was tucked into it, he popped his head up again and looked around, whimpering. When Grehssekker the Clown pushed his head down, the "volunteer's" big, belted belly rose above the top of the box. The illusionist pushed it down firmly and shut the top of the box on it. He made huge, comical gestures all around it, showing the audience all of its sides.

Sobs were heard from inside the box as Grehssekker went backstage and came out with an *enormous* hand saw. The illusionist gave a wicked grin, waved the saw threateningly, and pointed it at the box with the fearful volunteer inside. Pitiful wails came from the box as the illusionist began to saw through it. The wails faded to quiet sobs, then to silence as everybody watched the end of the saw lowering through the box. When it reached the bottom of the box, Grehssekker triumphantly opened the box along the place where he'd sawed through it. There were now two smaller boxes, each too small for the portly man he'd put in there.

Grehssekker swept his hands together to indicate that the trick was complete, but the audience called out for him to "bring him back." Grehssekker the Clown shook his head violently and then spread his hands helplessly. The audience laughingly insisted. Finally, he turned to the smaller boxes and put them together into one big one. He turned back to the crowd. Okay? He asked with gestures and raised eyebrows. "No," they called. "Bring him back."

He paced back and forth, flapping his huge shoes with each step. He sat on the ground and put his head in his hands despairingly. Finally, he stood and opened the box from the top. He moved to one side and with a grand gesture, he summoned the portly man to come out of the box. Nothing happened.

Good natured boos rose from the people, and Jenny, Rell and Mahlee joined in enthusiastically. The clown looked into the box, turned it on its side, turned it over and shook it. Still nothing. He began to sob dramatically and silently and tore wildly at his clown hair.

At last, the voice of a child rose above the crowd noise. "There he is!"

All eyes turned in the direction of the child's pointed finger and saw the portly gentleman at the far side of the tent, behind the audience, waving cheerily at everyone. The applause was uproarious.

After enjoying the cheers for a while, Grehssekker rolled out a small cannon and started gesturing over it. Jenny wondered what would get shot out of it. It was much too small to shoot a person into a net across the tent like she'd seen on TV. She turned and checked to make sure there *was* a net at the back of the tent.

There wasn't.

With a final flourish and a silent "magic" word, white flame burst forth from the cannon and circled around the tent, apparently without any destination. Jenny was startled to realize that as it passed over the hole in the central fenced area, it seemed to lurch a bit, and flashes of color appeared to spark there for a moment before it went on its zigzagging way. Nobody else seemed to have noticed.

The first stop it made was above Jenny herself, where, to Little Bee's delight, it circled her head several times before zooming off toward Rell. He caught it in both hands and bounced it up and down a few times, then tossed it away while he blew on his fingers a bit, laughing.

A sudden clackety clamor interrupted the proceedings as the white flame circled. A flock of dragon bats entered the tent on one side, detoured around the hole in the center, and then flapped on out the other side.

Some of the campers looked up at them and shrugged. Others ignored them altogether. This apparently was nothing new or alarming to them. The flame still wriggled around over everyone's heads until, with a decisive move, it landed just a bit above Mahlee and formed itself into a wide brimmed hat. It tipped at an angle over one of her eyes in a way that looked quite dashing. She rolled her eyes up, grinning, and after a moment she reached up and took the "hat" by its brim with the tips of her fingers. She held it in front of her and quickly blew on it, sending it back to Grehssekker, who grabbed it and stuffed it back into the cannon.

By then, the whole audience was laughing heartily. Jenny looked down at her side to laugh with Little Bee—who wasn't there.

Quickly she looked over to where Bee's parents were sitting, to see if the toddler had gone to them. She wasn't there either, and Jenny began to panic. Ahnie and Dohrwen had trusted her to watch out for Little Bee, but Jenny looked around the big tent twice before she saw her.

It was *not* a relief!

Chapter 14

◆

The Very, Very, Very Deep Hole

Little Bee was *inside of* the constantly changing fence with the warning sign about the very, very, very deep hole. She was squatting on the very edge of the hole, cradling a baby "dragon bat," crooning at it like a little mama. The very new-looking dragonet must have fallen from the flock that had just clattered overhead.

In moments Jenny had leaped over the fence, and was standing next to her little friend. She picked Little Bee up gently, with the dragonet still held tenderly in her tiny hands. By this time Ahnie and Dohrwen were there, right outside the fence, and Jennifer handed her over to them.

That's when she realized, that, right where she stood, the dirt was crumbling under her feet, and into *the hole!* She reached for the weird fence to pull herself from danger, but it had moved from where she grabbed, and Jennifer fell back into the hole along with the crumbling dirt.

I felt as if she was falling slowly, twisting in awkward circles, but unlike Alice's rabbit hole, there was absolutely nothing to look at or grab on the way down. There was only white dirt falling all around her but, when she slammed into the very bottom, she knew her fall hadn't been at all slow.

Jennifer wasn't sure how long she lay there, stunned. The first thing that came into focus for her was the sight of Atta Girl and Beauregard looking down at her. Jenny warned them away from the edge of the hole, for fear they'd come tumbling down on top of her. Atta mentally assured her they were too light, and too agile, for that to happen. Without taking her eyes off of Jennifer, Atta warned away the people who were starting to crowd in with them beside the hole. They moved back and Atta Girl wasn't heard from again. She was totally focused on Jenny, at the bottom of the hole. The campers held a meeting to decide how to get Jennifer out of there without collapsing the hole.

Meanwhile, Jenny took inventory of herself. She decided that, thankfully, nothing was broken, but she *felt* covered with bruises. The ones she could see were rapidly swelling, and she was, for the moment, grateful that she couldn't see the ghastly colors they would have been turning if she were on Earth.

She laid her head down again, hearing the voices above her in earnest discussion. The sounds were muffled, like a loud television program in the house next door. From time to time she could hear slightly raised words like, "No, that won't work, because ..." and "We've got to get her out of there, safely!" And then there was Little Bee's voice sobbing her name, and Ahnii's voice, hopefully reassuring her little one that Jenny would be saved.

Serious pain was gathering in Jenny as the shock of the fall wore off. She tried to get her mind off of it by looking around her. As she'd already suspected, the bottom of the hole was every bit as boring as the sides of it had been, except for a funny-looking rock that lay half buried, or maybe even deeper than that, in the dirt at the very center of the hole, about a foot away from her right hand. The part that she could see was in small cubes linked at the corners, but she couldn't really focus on the cubes, because there seemed to be so many corners shimmering in and around it. She noticed that even though the rock was dusted with the dirt from the bottom of the hole, there was something different about it ... although she couldn't focus on the shape of the rock, at times parts of it gleamed brightly through the dirt that clung to it. She just lay there for a bit, dreading the added pain of moving. But after she thought about it for a minute or two, her curiosity won out. She reached out for the rock, pulling the much larger part of it up out of the ground, where it had been hidden.

The moment she had it in her hand, though, she knew it had been a mistake.

Instantly, she dropped the strange stone as if it were hot, and as she did that, the sides of the hole that surrounded her faded away, though they didn't disappear completely. The good news was that she didn't hurt anymore. The bad news was, she couldn't feel *anything*, anymore! At first she thought she was numb, but soon realized that it wasn't that. It wasn't just that she was numb, because even though things around her had faded, she could still see them. What she couldn't see was herself; her hands, her legs, her clothing. Anything.

She didn't panic, not even when she finally realized that she didn't feel anything, and that she wasn't anything—anywhere!

I must be dead, she thought, and her thoughts went to those above the hole, trying to get her out. All they would find, if they finally succeeded, was her body.

My body! she thought then. *I can see everything else, even though it's dim, but I can't see my body! It isn't down here. At least I can't see it, whether I'm in it, or not. I wonder if Atta can see me … or hear me?* She'd already realized she couldn't hear Atta anymore, although her cat's friend, Beauregard Lion, was still staring into the hole too, and becoming more and more agitated. Atta Girl seemed to be in a kind of trance, staring intently at something Jennifer couldn't see. She wondered what it could possibly be that Atta was focusing on.

She was trying to adjust to this new situation when she realized that, as she thought about the people above her, she was slowly rising up through the hole, until she seemed to herself to be standing on air a few inches above the level of the ground around it. She quickly thought about being *away* from that hole, and as she thought it, she moved over the ground to, and then through, the undulating fence.

"Want Jenny!" Little Bee's sad voice reached Jenny once again, and as she heard it she was there, hoping somehow to reassure her little friend. But Little Bee couldn't see or hear her either. *Nobody could.*

Grehssekker was addressing the crowd that had gathered around him to discuss how to get Jennifer out of the hole. First, they tried to persuade

Atta Girl to let them know how Jenny was doing at the bottom of the hole. She didn't respond, though, not even to Beau. She still was concentrating on something no one else could see or hear. The group gave up on that, and turned to trying out ideas for rescuing Jenny from the hole.

Mahlee paced with agitation at the edge of the group and called out, "Hasn't *anybody* got a ladder?"

Rell, sitting cross-legged directly in front of the Illusionist, stood up, standing with his small fists on his hips, "Yeah, where's a ladder? That's *Jennifer Arthur* down there, the Dreamsaver herself. That's *Jenny!*"

Grehssekker reached down and absent-mindedly removed a couple of coins from Rell's hair as he asked around, but nobody knew of a long enough ladder. "And anyway," Dohrwen commented, "we can't go close enough to the hole to drop one in, without the hole collapsing even more. There is the danger that the person setting the ladder would fall and more dirt, and even the ladder and the person, would fall in on Jenny, perhaps burying her alive."

Alive? Jenny thought. *I don't think that will happen.*

"True, true." Grehssekker agreed with Dohrwen; the others nodded, silent for long moments.

"What about a very strong fishing rod with a very long pole?" asked the roly-poly cook. No one had anything like that, and obviously they couldn't just fish Jenny up anyway.

"Oh, that poor girl," Mahlee's friend Jhinlillee wailed. She began to weep noisily, and Grehssekker pulled a silky white kerchief from his sleeve, which was followed by one scarf after another, attached to one another, somehow, invisibly. He handed her the first one, then took the last one to dab at his own sudden tears.

Jenny was moved by their concern but unable to reassure them, or even herself. She wandered away from the meeting and moved around the campground. She saw then that the pathways that led out of it could no longer be seen. There were just foggy areas where the elusive paths might have been. After a time of moving aimlessly, smelling food she couldn't eat, and hearing conversations she couldn't get into, she realized she was not even able to shed the tears that she absolutely *needed* to cry.

She thought again about those misty paths. Maybe she could actually find a way out of there. Maybe she could even set up a trail, somehow, for the others to follow.

But which path would be best? And should she leave this place where everyone knew her? Or had known her.

She looked back at Atta Girl, Rell, Mahlee Kahdel and all the campers who had welcomed them so generously only yesterday. She moved once more toward Little Bee, who was now sobbing quietly. Not even Little Bee could sense her presence. She had no idea whether she could accomplish anything by leaving, but she had to go. Staying like this, not able to touch or talk to or even be seen by anyone just hurt too much.

Goodbye, she wished them all. *Goodbye and blessings, everyone.*

Chapter 15

Memory Rooms

Jennifer turned back to the pathways. *Eeny, meeny, miney mo,* she recited to herself. It was the counting rhyme she and her friends had used to choose "it" when she was just a kid, back in California. That was when she was still young enough to play such games.

She started the count over again a few times, because the pathway openings kept changing places. Finally she simply focused on one of them and hurried through the opening before it could disappear.

Once she'd entered the foggy passageway the air cleared, but she thought at first that leaves were falling from the trees that arched above the passage. Before long, though, she realized that the things falling were strings—some long, some short. The strings glowed as if with an inner light, moving without falling—drifting, knotting, and unknotting in always-changing patterns.

She tried to move her legs faster to speed her way. Even though she couldn't see her body, she still felt as if she had one. But she couldn't hurry, because her legs still didn't touch the ground or floor to give her traction.

She gave that up and let herself be moved through the tunnel toward whatever her destination was. As she moved on, there were more and more strings around her, and she brought up her invisible hands to clear them away from her face. To her surprise, it worked. The strings "saw" her body, clinging to it in places; they were not passing through her as other things had.

In the widest part of the passage, ribbons of color appeared in the mix of strings. Soon they were crowding the strings out and floating everywhere, weaving in and out of each other and clinging, as the strings had, to where Jenny's body seemed to be. When the ribbons moved around her, they caused a light tingle where they touched, and their dancing was lovely. In her imagination, Jenny danced with them.

As she moved among the strings and ribbons, Jenny became aware of other presences brushing by her as if they might be somebody's passing thoughts, but not hers. If they had anything to do with her, she didn't sense *that*.

The ribbons continued to glow softly, tenderly brushing against what she thought of as herself; that is, brushing or clinging to all the places where she thought her body would be. She let go of her invisible body to float and slowly turn in the tunnel space, which was filled with the streaming colors and presences. She didn't try anymore to figure out what they meant.

She allowed her mind to float too, and let herself feel the glorious colors and the mysterious presences that surrounded her. Suddenly she thought that if she were dead, then this must be heaven, or at least a suburb of it. And maybe the presences brushing her were angels. *This wouldn't be too bad, but an eternity of it? Excuse me, God, but this will soon be booorrring!*

As the last thought rose in her mind, she felt herself turned upright, and she was gently dumped into a room that seemed familiar, though at first she didn't know why.

She brushed off the few vivid ribbons of light that still clung to her and looked carefully around the room. It had corner windows like her room at home, but she couldn't see through them. In another corner was a bassinette, shirred with layers of sheer fabric in soft colors, and beside it was a wooden rocker, like the one in her room at home, but the cushions were a different color and pattern. Mom once told her, "take good care of that rocker, because I plan to rock my grandchildren in it."

There were other vague shapes in the room that seemed to be other pieces of furniture, though she found she couldn't focus on them.

Small sounds were coming from the bassinette, and Jenny moved toward it and peered in. There was a baby there, stirring and stretching with sweet waking-up sounds. *Maybe this is one of the missing children* she thought hopefully. If it was, she'd found it. *But now what?* She knew she wasn't anywhere on the White World, because of the colors. She remembered the day when Mom brought Warren home from the hospital. He'd been sooo cute!

She heard someone coming, and the baby did too. It turned its head toward the sound and cooed happily, just before Mom came into the room!

Oh, Mom, you look so beautiful, and so young! Well, if Warren was in the bassinette, Mom would be twelve years younger than she was when Jenny had last seen her. *Funny,* she thought, *how we think we remember things in the past, but we don't really. When I get back home … I'll start a journal.*

Her thoughts were quickly interrupted when Dad came into the room! He looked like Dad, of course, but he was also *so* young—just a kid, almost!

Mom looked up at him, smiling, and handed him the baby. "Isn't she precious, dear?"

She! Jenny took another look at the smiling little one. *Could it be …?*

"Who but our sweet Jennifer would wake up in the morning smiling?" Mom continued, tucking the little crib blanket more securely around the baby's shoulders.

Herself!

"She almost never cries."

Jenny turned away, although they wouldn't see her tears anyway. She knew she was crying but she couldn't feel the tears. After a moment she turned back and gently "touched" her infant self's tiny hand, which seemed to curl around her finger. *Baby me,* she said gently, *don't ever forget how lucky you are to have such a wonderful family. And when you get a bit older, be very, very careful around the lilac tree in our backyard.*

She went back to the passageway. This wasn't *her* time. She didn't belong here.

Chapter 16

A Friend!

Jennifer dove into the passageway headfirst, because it made her feel as if she were more in control of her destination. She tried swimming, but even though she was making the motions, she couldn't tell if it made her move any faster. Then the gleaming bits of strings became lighted ribbons again, and finally that's all there were. Either she was getting somewhere, or the passageway itself was changing. Just to be on the safe side, she stood up again as the ribbons thinned out to make room for white strings again, just moments before she came back out into the campground.

It was nighttime there—time for the nightly starstorms. White World stars were zipping and zapping all around and through her, without her feeling anything. She could hear snores coming from the campsites, and she thought, once, that she heard Little Bee cry out in her sleep.

The zinging star missiles whistled through her, and she wondered again how, if she wasn't really there to everything and everyone else, the glowing strings and ribbons still brushed against her and clung to her, but not through her. They helped, though, to strengthen her feeling of actually *having* a body, even though that body seemed pretty much not there.

She stood for a while, listening to all the night sounds; crickets, or whatever passed for crickets on this world, and starstorm winds roaring through the trees. She saw whirling stars of all sizes—from the size of the diamond in Mom's ring to a melon-sized star, like the one which could easily have killed her the first time she was on this world. Morgan the Wonderful Wohtt had risked his own life to save her, tackling her to throw her out of the star's path and covering her with himself to shield her against more of them, while she was still face down on the ground and too shocked to get up again.

She wondered if the Wohtt was still in the dangerous hands of the Ghanglers.

When she had first returned to this world and witnessed Morgan being wohtt-napped by Ghanglers, as she'd watched it looked as if he'd slipped out of his chains, but after that something rippled through the scene, and she hadn't been able to see anything more. But if he'd escaped, where was he? She wondered if her family had missed her yet, or if time had once again done its trick, letting all this happen while no time went by on Earth.

And what was the good of a body that couldn't be seen and couldn't touch anything except for silly strings and ribbons? She couldn't even feel those, except for an occasional tingle, but those apparently could feel and touch her. So what use was she in the search for all the gone? She supposed that by now, her own name would be added to that missing persons list. Instead of being a searcher, she was now one of the gone.

Finally her frustrating thoughts wound down. She went into Ahnii's and Dohrwen's wagon and curled up next to sleeping Little Bee to rest awhile. It wasn't that her body was tired, or that the stars might hurt her. It was just that she felt *so* lonely!

When morning came, she left everyone in the campground to their breakfasting and picked another passageway. This time, she found a birthday party on the other side; it was her very own birthday. She knew it was her sixth, because there were six candles on the dragon-shaped cake Mom had baked and decorated for her. There was Warren, sitting at the long table next to her. He'd have been two-years old at that time, and he was just as cuddly and cute as she remembered him. And there

were her friends, Ruth, Gracie, Delores, Kate, and six-year-old Willa—
still her very best friend!

The dangers of the last White World visit weren't quite as terrifying
as this one, because Willa had been there with her as well as Atta Girl.
Atta Girl was on the White World this time too, but she definitely wasn't
with her now. Her dear cat was back in the campground, still in some
kind of a trance by day, and sleeping under Little Bee's wagon all night
long, not even twitching a whisker as Jenny passed by.

It was getting harder and harder to look at her past, but she figured
that was what she was supposed to do, or things wouldn't be set up this
way. Only how could this help her find the missing children, or Morgan,
or even the powerful chrystal that was needed for her to get home?

She went in and out of several more passageways. The memory
rooms were always different, although Jenny thought sometimes that
she'd gone into a room she'd entered before. She visited her violin concert
in the ninth grade, when she was soloist and first chair of the school
orchestra. She was pretty proud of herself there and thought that ninth-
grade Jenny played the violin very well—for a ninth grader. She wished
again that she'd started keeping a journal as soon as she could write.
Memories are so precious, and so *many* are dimmed or lost.

She dropped by to watch recess at her elementary school. There she
was, climbing on the bars, hanging upside down, red-faced, and laughing.
She was wearing jeans and a T-shirt. She'd been glad she didn't have
to do what Grandma had to do before playing on the bars. Grandma
had told her that in *her* day she'd had to wear dresses with little ruffled
panties over her underpants. They were made of the same material as
her dresses, so they wouldn't look like underwear. Pants, for girls, were
against the rules in Grandma's day. Yuck!

Jennifer scarcely thought about the passageways as they took her
from room to room. She had to admit, though, that they were a relaxing
way to travel. It began to seem routine to go from one revisited memory
to another, with brief stops at the campground in between.

She visited a picnic that she and Willa had when they were both in
elementary school. That was when she was terrified of heights. Even so,

she'd made it all the way up to Willa's tree house for the picnic, in spite of the cold sweat that broke out on her forehead with the effort, and the view of their whole neighborhood and beyond was *fab!*

In another room, she and her family were flying kites on the Marina Green near San Francisco's Fisherman's Wharf. The sky was filled with the most amazing kites she had *ever* seen. Her own kite was a dragon with a five foot wing span. Warren's was a pirate ship with all sails full. They'd found them in a Pier 39 kite shop. It had been a wonderful day. She sat invisibly on a nearby bench and watched, laughed, and ached with homesickness. Finally she *had* to move on to the next destination.

She stayed only briefly in the next several scenes; her first day in kindergarten, Warren's christening day, and her graduation from ninth grade to high school, just a few months before what she thought of as *now*.

Then there were scenes of the town's historic Carnegie Library, where she'd found her first Oz book and realized with delight that there were *lots* more of them.

It was even harder to watch when she, Willa and another neighbor friend were playing Monopoly at the kitchen table in Jennifer's house. Warren wanted to play too, but Jenny told him to "bug off, kid." Jenny hadn't been looking at him then, but her invisible self did. As she looked on now she saw his hurt look as he walked away with his head down and his hands in his pockets, and now she might *never* have a chance to make it up to him. She might never have a chance to tell him she was sorry.

But the scene after that was the real shocker. It was in her own high school's auditorium; her whole class was graduating. Then she saw that one of the graduates was herself, in cap and gown. Her hair was longer than she wore it now, and she was wearing high heels. Even so, it was herself, only ... she wouldn't be graduating for almost three more years!

So, she mused, *if I graduate, then I must not be dead after all. But no one anywhere can see or hear me. I can't even see myself. If I'm not dead, then what am I?* She leaned wearily into the passageway back to the campground, thinking maybe she'd just have to try harder; she would just *make* them see and hear her.

When she was back in the campground she located Rell, scuffing around the campsite and kicking up dust. She walked right up to him and hollered at the top of what should have been her voice, *I'm here, Rell. Try hard! You can see me.* The problem was, she had no voice, and Rell walked glumly right through her.

She found Atta, who was back into her daytime trance. She touched her in her favorite scratch spot behind her right ear. The little ear flicked, and Beauregard looked at his friend hopefully, but that was all. Nothing had really changed.

Without much hope, she moved toward the middle of the camp area, but not near the hole in the center of it. An extra fence had been built out beyond the other one. This one was taller and didn't move up and down.

"Hey! Hey, everybody! It's me, Jennifer Arthur! Doesn't *anybody* hear me?" Her words didn't make even a dent in the sounds and voices all around her.

She sighed, and randomly chose another passageway. This one was even thicker than the others with those squirmy strings. They knotted and unknotted as she passed through them, and the way seemed longer than the other ways had been. The passage itself had unexpected turns and twists in it; and it stayed white, the strands of light staying stringy for such a long time that Jenny was considering whether she should turn around and go back the way she came.

But what's the point of that? She asked herself. *I'd be as alone there as I am in this squirmy tunnel.*

In that passage, the strings of light were still strings—no color-radiating light ribbons dancing around her, so she was unprepared when she was dumped into another memory, this one from her first time on the White World. This scene recalled the time when she, Willa, and Atta Girl were accompanied by their very first White World friend, Morgan the Wonderful, Wandering Wohtt to the cave of Nitty Gritty the Newfangler. It was late, and Morgan had warned them against traveling at night, but they assured him they weren't afraid of the dark. They'd wanted to get as far away from the horrible, whirlwind-walking Ghanglers as possible, and as quickly as they could.

How could they have known, then, that nights on the White World were so different from nights on Earth? Here, the nights are as white as the days, and when the thick night mists gather everywhere, "stars" come slicing through them, perilous to anything or anyone foolish enough to be outdoors at these times.

Small stars had stung and sizzled at first, then a walnut-sized one had slammed against Jenny's head, leaving a lump and a trickle of white blood where it hit.

The time this memory was replaying was when Jenny hadn't noticed a melon-sized star zapping right at her, and Morgan, that *Wonderful*, Wandering Wohtt, had run back to tackle her and knock her out of the way. Then he'd covered her until she could get up again, even though he himself was protected only by his fragile, dandelion-like fluff.

She felt weepy again. These memories only made her sadder and even more confused about their purpose. If they were to teach her a lesson, what good would it do when she couldn't relate to anyone—not even the silent presences that floated past?

Apparently these dim presences either couldn't, or wouldn't, see or notice her.

An instant later though, her loneliness burst into sparkling stars, rockets, and joy-tears as she realized one of the presences *did* notice her and drew closer. And she noticed it back, and—somehow—knew who it was, even though she didn't know how she knew.

Chapter 17

Trapped

The moment Jennifer and Morgan's invisible fingers touched, all the sounds and movements of the memory rooms and the in-between tunnels were suddenly motionless and silent. A star the size of a tennis ball was lodged partway into Jenny's shoulder, where it had stopped. She'd left it there, because it made no difference how she looked when nobody could see her. Now though, as she grasped Morgan's barely sensed hand with one of hers she tried to brush the awkward star from her shoulder. It wouldn't budge so she backed away from it, still holding Morgan's hand, and that worked. The star was still poised midair where it had been, as motionless as everything else.

Although she and Morgan still couldn't speak to each other, Jenny could very faintly see him. And, just as faintly, she could now see herself. They were only dimly visible against the motionless background as moving, shimmering figures, as clear as spring water. But they *could* be seen!

As if they had talked it over and agreed on it, Jennifer and the Wohtt moved together to reenter what they both felt was the return passage. For some reason, the way back to the camp seemed much longer than the one Jenny had taken to get there. There were even more zigzags in it, with sharp corners around which the two of them seemed to be dragged, careening through the glowing white strings and ribbons, so that their nearly invisible figures seemed almost solid, with ribbons clinging all over them and trailing raggedly behind.

In what she guessed was about the center of the passage, they encountered colored ribbons again, this time they as brilliant as neon lights. When they brushed against where Jenny figured her body was, they pressed tightly against her and, it seemed, against Morgan. While they moved among them Jenny felt their tingling warmth in her body but also a sort of *tugging* sensation pulling backward on her feet. Still holding hands, she and the Wohtt pushed their way forward, kicking against the ribbons with Morgan in the lead. At last they came into white strings again as the colored ribbons disappeared. These strings clung so stubbornly to Jenny and Morgan that they were kept busy frantically pulling them away from their hands and faces.

They continued to move in the direction they thought of as forward, though, until Morgan's telepathic message came to her: *They're not strings anymore, Jennifer. They're fingers now, trying to pry our hands apart.*

At the same time Jennifer, shuddering with feelings of doom, answered him: *The tunnel is shrinking, Morgan! It's closing in on us!*

The worst part was that walls were closing off *between* them too. The weird string-fingers were working harder and harder to pull them apart, and the ribbons seemed determined to drag Jenny backward.

"Bite them!" she urged Morgan, almost frightened to hear her voice out loud again, even though it was very soft—much quieter than her usual voice. "Bite those fingers!" She herself nipped at the ones she could reach and kicked with all her strength against those that were trying to drag her back.

"Bite them?" Morgan said reluctantly.

Jenny remembered that he was one of at least two universes' most peaceful persons. She *had* to convince him.

"Don't bite them *off*, Morgan. Just nip them enough to make them stop. Please!"

The tunnel walls were still closing in between them. The opening was now barely large enough for her to fit through. "Please, Morgan! It's my only chance!"

The fingers began to make rapid squealing sounds and, one by one as both Jenny and Morgan nipped at them, they dropped away. At the same time Jenny kicked off the ribbons pulling her back. Turning herself sideways to fit through the shrinking hole, with a last-minute squeeze and a firm tug from the Wohtt, Jenny was through and out with Morgan. They'd hoped they were sensing the exit ahead of them, and then suddenly they were there, still almost invisible, back in the campground from which Jenny had fled, time and time again, into her own memories. Sighing, she resumed plucking the strings and ribbons from her now barely visible body.

Morgan was already almost free of his.

Chapter 18

The Purr Wins Out

That same morning, there'd been great excitement in the camp. Nitty Gritty the Newfangler had arrived unexpectedly through one of the passageways, and the passage she came through was no longer fogged over. The mists that blocked the other passages were thinning out, too.

Instead of her usual jeans and lab coat, Nitty wore a silvery kaftan that stirred in the gentle breeze, while her long platinum hair floated free of her usual headband. Briefly, she greeted the now-wide-awake Atta Girl and waved general greetings to the campers before asking them to step back, assuring them that there were things that must be done immediately.

From the large bag she carried she produced two obviously heavy, thick-sided boxes and set their tops beside them about five feet apart on a nearby empty picnic table. Then she dug into it again, pulling out a peculiar tool, something like a fishing pole, but metallic, and apparently mechanical. At one end it had a double-clawed attachment like oversized salad tongs, only deeper and more businesslike. Nitty operated its open-and-close mechanism from the handle to be sure it was working. She moved as close to the very, very, very deep hole as seemed safe, and then she extended the rod to a position where its other end was just over the hole's center. She leaned forward against the new fence to operate controls that released a rope which extended straight down as she wound it out, until the feel of it told her it had reached the hole's bottom. She maneuvered the tongs from knobs at her end until she felt something catch in the claw's cage. Hopefully, she reeled her catch up and over to herself. The tongs brought with them a large, odd-looking chrystal. Wearing gloves, Jenny plucked it out of the tongs and positioned it to drop in the larger box on the table. The chrystal she had earlier "borrowed back" from Atta Girl was already gleaming in the smaller box.

Mahlee Kahdel moved up next to her with Rell close beside her. "'Scuze me, Miz Gritty," the guide said, "but I be *that* worried about our Jennifer. The Rememberer hisself put the Dreamsaver in my personal care. Will them there rocks help us find her, ma'am?"

"I are right worried too, ma'am." Rell put in. "I be a personal friend of Jennifer's, and of her brother Warren, sort of."

"'Tis glad I am to see that Jenny hath such loyal friends," Nitty said. "Although these chrystals will not help us to *find* Jennifer, when she *is* found they shalt be absolutely needful to bring her back to us."

Mahlee, Rell, and the rest of the gathered campers were silent, trying to imagine why, if they found Jenny, they would need these strange rocks to "bring her back" to them.

Everyone held their breath as Nitty prepared to drop the large chrystal into the larger box. Instead of dropping though, it suddenly lifted in a sparking arc to a few feet above a place halfway to the smaller chrystal, and the smaller chrystal sent its own arc up to meet it, where they met in the middle with a sudden small explosion. Everyone jumped back, away from the fireworks. Even the Newfangler inched back a cautious step.

At the place where the two arcs met in the middle, there was a sudden loud *snap* before the sizzling chrystals settled back into their own boxes, and then Jennifer's very best friend, Willa Walker, suddenly stood on the table where the sparks had met. Finding herself abruptly in front of a large crowd of strangers, Willa felt as awkward and confused as she could ever remember being.

Nitty gasped, "Willa?" and hurried to greet her, but when Grehssekker heard Willa's name exclaimed he was more than equal to that momentous occasion.

In a grand manner, he held up his hand to Willa to help her down from the table as he dramatically announced to the crowd, "Ladees and Gents, we have yet another celebrity in our midst—another to whom all of us citizens of the White World owe our deepest gratitude."

Nitty Gritty hugged Willa, and with one arm around the girl's waist she waited with an amused smile for Grehssekker to finish his speech. "We are privileged," he continued, "to welcome Willa Walker, the *third* Dreamsaver, into our midst—in person." He bowed in a courtly manner to the nervous teenager and the crowd erupted into cheers, pressing happily forward to shake Willa's hand or hug her. Freshly baked pastries and other goodies were quietly brought from the various tents and trailers and set on the picnic tables to celebrate this special happening.

Before they could deal with food, though, Nitty Gritty had questions to answer, including Willa's hardest question of all. "I see Atta Girl," she said to Nitty, "but where is Jenny?" The crowd held its collective breath as everyone strained to hear what Nitty would answer.

The Newfangler was about to explain what she knew or guessed about the situation, when a stir of excitement swept the crowd, and Little Bee's voice carried across it, "Jenny? *My* Jenny?"

At first all Nitty and the others noticed was a snarl of glowing strings and ribbons that were falling to the ground out of midair into small heaps. But those strands that were still suspended clung to nearly imperceptible forms. The forms themselves looked to be about as solid as heat waves over hot pavement, but they were *shapes!*

"Jennifer?" Nitty called wonderingly as, leading the crowd, she approached the spot, and then …"*Morgan?*"

With a sound like something between a purr and a growl, Atta Girl had already bounded to the place where strings and ribbons were falling.

The purr won out.

Chapter 19

Another Arrival

Before anything else, Jenny and Morgan's solidifying had been the very first thing Nitty Gritty took care of after they had moved toward her hesitantly, like wary ghosts. Their dim, mummy-like forms still trailed glowing white strands.

In the midst of the excited crowd, Jenny welcomed the sudden exhaustion she felt. At least it was a *feeling!* The fatigue and sleeplessness that her invisible body hadn't been able to feel now spilled back into her all at once.

The Newfangler softly shushed the eager and bewildered campers—even Willa and Atta Girl —gesturing them back from Jenny and Morgan. She was worried that the two might be overwhelmed before they could regain their strength. She led them over to the boxes on the table. Jenny glanced inside and recognized the smaller of the two rocks; it was the same strange, cube-like chrystal, which had been dangling from Atta Girl's collar. In the other box she saw one like it, only much larger. That one, she realized, was the one that had drawn her into such a frighteningly strange world—a world that existed alongside the White World she knew well, but where she was unable to touch or be touched by anything about it.

What a great "searcher" she had been, Jennifer thought sadly. When she'd had the missing chrystal in her hand she had dropped it, without recognizing it.

And she hadn't really "found" Morgan, either—the Wonderful Wohtt had actually found *her*. And as far as the missing children were concerned, she had no idea whether any or all of them had already been found while she was floundering around with strings and ribbons. Though she had learned a few things about herself while she was there, she had basically been busy going in circles in tunnels and finding nothing at all.

"Touch the smaller stone lightly, then the larger one," Nitty told her, interrupting the silent scolding Jenny had been giving herself. "Then you do it, Morgan."

Touch them?! Jenny absolutely trusted the Newfangler, but she *didn't* trust those weird rocks.

"'Tis fine, Jennifer," Nitty assured her. She couldn't really hear Jenny's words, yet, but Jennifer's reluctance to touch the stone was obvious. "T'was that smaller stone that Atta had on her collar all this time, and it gave her no trouble at all. This large one is the one which set you on your wild journey. It is the other side of the gate, the side which balances it. Thou needst not pick either of them up. Merely touch the small one first, then give the large one only an itty bitty touch, to normalize any possible bummer effect of the first. Together, these two doth balance and complete the Chrystal Gate."

While Jennifer still hesitated, Morgan moved forward and touched the stones with his own long, slender fingertips. Before her very eyes, Jennifer saw the Wohtt becoming more and more solid and more and more *himself*. Although she was still fearful, she followed his example, reaching out and touching first the small stone then and then, still trembling, touching the large one.

With those touches, Jennifer also felt herself coming back to herself, marveling over her recovering ability to touch, feel, and move things, and to be seen and heard again. The two no-longer-gone travelers were eager to find out from Nitty what had happened that led her to find them. They were eager but, almost overcoming that, they were exhausted.

"Jenny, *Jenny!*" Little Bee's voice cut through the awed murmur of the stranded campers; "Bee wants *Jenny!*" When Little Bee had squirmed her way through the crowd to get to her, Jenny lifted the toddler up in her arms for a hug while Atta Girl, ignoring Nitty's warnings to stay back, spooled around her legs. As soon as Jenny could ease herself away from them, she gave the Newfangler, Rell, and Mahlee hugs, as well. Fuzzily, she wondered if she really had seen Willa back in the crowd?

"How did you know where to find us?" Morgan asked the Newfangler. Apparently he was too tired for his usual alliterations.

"Yes, Nitty," Jennifer added. "None of us here in the campground could find a way out. How did *you* find a way in? How did you even know I was lost?"

"Oh, thou canst not credit me for that, dear Jennifer. 'Twas Atta Girl who didst show me."

"Atta?" Jennifer looked down at her dear cat with wonder. The powder from the brush Nitty had given Atta was now just small patches of white and her honey-orange fur glowed through like flames in the all-white surroundings. "If you knew the way out of here," Jenny asked her cat in bewilderment, "why didn't you tell me? Why didn't you tell *anybody*?"

I didn't knowww. Nittyyy did, Atta answered, leaning hard against Jenny's legs. As usual, she was a cat of few words.

"That be not entirely true," The Newfangler said with a slight smile. "I did not know the *way*, but verily, I didst know *how*, thanks be to this super-duper feline."

"How did that happy happenstance occur?" Morgan asked, yawning through his again alliterated words.

"Art thou certain thou dost want to hear that now, dear Friend Wohtt, before thou dost rest?"

"Well, I sure want to hear it, Nitty," Jenny interrupted, struggling to keep her itchy eyes open. "*How* did you know how?"

Nitty began, "Well, I was passing through Nindenscirre Shire, searching yet for the missing children, when suddenly Atta Girl mind-screamed at me that you'd fallen. She was still looking down the hole as I felt her scream, so that I didst find myself able to see, through her eyes, as thou didst pick up the chrystal at the hole's bottom. And then you disappeared."

As Nitty spoke, she gently directed the two who had been lost into a pair of rocking chairs that she had requested, waiting nearby. The chairs belonged to a stranded merchant who'd been delivering them to a customer on the far side of the Wandering Waters. Nitty quietly reassured him that he would be well compensated for them, and he'd cheerfully agreed.

"I didst inquire of Atta where thou wert, Jenny, and she didst reply that she did not know, that you were simply gone. So I told her to keep her mind firmly with mine, except for eating and sleeping times, whilst I wouldst be able to continue to focus on her, and go from there to find thee. Morgan's presence was a slamwow surprise when I didst arrive … "Jennifer, dost thou know how wonderful it was that you found him, even in another dimension?"

Jenny had heard the first part of Nitty's story, but most of it became part of her dream—a dream about ribbon-filled tunnels, invisibility, and memories. Later, Nitty Gritty would tell her the story again.

As she was drawn more deeply into sleep, Jennifer mumbled, "I didn't find him, Nitty. *He* found *me.*"

During the discussion, Atta Girl had quietly occupied Jenny's lap, and Beauregard, unwilling to be far from Atta, fit himself into Jenny's chair too, between Atta and the rocker's armrest.

After several minutes when Nitty Newfangler was sure that both of the returned travelers were soundly sleeping, she gently removed Atta and the lion from Jenny's chair, assuring them that they would be with Jenny again soon. She took two silky scarves from her round-handled traveling bag and used them to securely belt the two sleepers into place in the rockers. Then she drew a couple of smallish gadgets from the same bag and fastened them to the bottoms of the chair seats. At this point, her wonderful, platinum hair and silvery caftan stirred and glowed even more brightly while she started the chairs slowly rocking.

When both Jenny and Morgan were deeply asleep, the rocking became more and more vigorous. Although the chairs were still steady enough not to alarm the sleepers, they began to rise into the air. The campers whispered with quiet wonder as they watched the sleeping Jenny and Morgan rise up in them.

Their whispers grew louder with thrilled amazement that the sleepers didn't hear. As the chairs rose the watchers realized that Jennifer's natural colors - her Earth colors - were slowly returning to her. When they finally lost sight of the rocking chairs, the awed crowd began to disperse quietly to their separate shelters. The night mists were beginning to waft around them.

Nitty left the stones and her other equipment on the table. She needed to rest a bit, too. "Wilt thou watch out for this stuff of mine, young man?" she asked Rell. He agreed enthusiastically, lingering there to watch and to reflect on the many wonders he'd seen since he launched his homemade raft to go adventuring. He hadn't felt even the tiniest of storming stars yet, so he sat on a bench attached to the table and leaned back against it. If the storming stars became dangerous, he resolved, he'd get *under* the table and watch out for Nitty Newfangler's chrystals from there. That's how it happened that, as he relaxed and remembered, he heard another *snap* from the arcing chrystals.

Chapter 20

Meeting After All

Rell was the only one who noticed when the chrystals arced again. He stared in awe at the boy who stood on the table where Willa had been just a few minutes before. The boy—who Rell thought was probably as much as thirteen years old—was looking with disgust at his left foot, which had landed in the middle of a white cherry pie. Gingerly, the stranger lifted his foot out of it, and, using one of the napkins stacked on the table, he stood stork-like on one foot and began cleaning pie filling off of his shoe.

He noticed Rell out of the corner of his eye and straightened.

"Hey, fella," the newcomer said, "that's a truly ferocious hat you've got."

"Ferocious?" Rell repeated. "Oh no, my hat really wouldn't hurt anyone."

"No, what I meant is that it's really cool."

Rell rolled his eyes upward to study his own hat. "I guess on a real hot day it does help keep me cool."

Warren chuckled, "I mean that your hat is great-looking. Is that a real plant growing on it?"

"Yes, but it be … *your* hat—that's truly ferocious!" Warren was wearing his prized Dr. Seuss hat, although the red stripes were only different textures of white stripes now. And so was he, he realized. So he must be on the White World at last. *Somewhere* on the White World!

"Hey, Cool Hat Luke," Warren began, as he started to climb off the table.

"'Er—th' name's Rell," the boy said nervously.

"Yeah." Warren grinned. "That was just a nickname I was giving you, until I could find out your real name." Rell grinned back, and Warren asked, "Hey, do you know where my sister is? Her name is Jenny."

"You're Jennifer's brother? You're Warren? Stormin' stars, I *knew* I was gonna like you." He reached up to Warren to help him down "My name's Rell. Hey, Warren, have you got any other great hats?"

"Yeah, I've got a few, but not with me."

"Well, I got a bunch of 'em in th' trailer I be stayin' in. I had some of 'em in my hobo bag and folks here have given me more, and I've made more since we been here. Y'wanna see 'em?"

"Sure thing, Rell. If that hat is any example, I'd *really* like to see what else you've got."

Rell hesitated. He *couldn't* leave until Nitty Newfangler returned to relieve him from his watch. Just then she returned, signaling a thank you to Rell and letting him know that he could leave. She nodded and smiled at Warren too, but of course she didn't recognize him. This was his very first time actually on the White World.

Chatting away like old pals and bypassing the crowd still huddled around Willa, the boys headed toward the trailer that held Rell's hat collection.

"I've just started this one," Rell said. The base of the hat was a wide brim made of some kind of broad leaves, stitched together. Warren was truly impressed. He only collected hats when he saw them in shops or consignment stores or garage sales. This guy *made* his.

The idea of making them from found stuff fascinated him, and the boys were so deep in conversation they missed everything when another stir of excitement caught the crowd's attention. All eyes but theirs turned to a place just in front of one of the pathway entrances, but the two boys were already lost in the inspection of Rell's remarkable hats.

Chapter 21

Scattered Celebrations

Jenny's dreams put her back into the strange rooms of memories, all tangled together with glowing ribbons and all of them white, even those that had been memories of Earth originally in color. The dream ribbons brushed her gently, at first. But then they wrapped around her and held her more and more firmly. The dream became a nightmare as the binding of the ribbons became tighter and tighter, and distant, excited voices grew louder and louder.

The dream seemed threatening at first, and Jennifer tore frantically at the white dream ribbons, so that she could protect herself from an approaching mob or at least try to run, but as she flailed about in her dream, she woke herself up and the voices were still there.

These voices, though, were cheering for her!

She stretched her arms and legs, waking up more as she looked below. The excited citizens cheered even louder when they saw that she was awake at last. She could only make out the word "Dreamsaver" from the jumble of shouts below.

From familiar landmarks, Jenny realized she and Morgan were still somewhere on the away side of Too Tall Mountain. And she could see *exactly* why the people below them were cheering.

Looking behind her, she saw that the two most prominent White World suns were lined up vertically, almost directly behind her. She turned forward again and looked down. Her shadow lay out large and long in front of and below her, but there were two things she didn't understand about it—first, there were *no* shadows on the White World, and second, *this* shadow was in Technicolor! Everything and everyone in her shadow was in full color too, and after a moment or two, she realized color was seeping out everywhere from wherever her shadow fell.

She herself, and her clothing, were in full, natural colors, as well. With glad tears stinging her eyes, she reached across the open space between herself and Morgan to wake him gently.

Even before he was fully awake she saw that he, too, had begun to blush with color. Oh, he was still mostly white, but iridescent pastel colors lit the tips of his fluff, and his arms and legs were a rich, creamy color. He was still her dear friend Morgan, though, and now, since she'd touched him, he also had a shadow on the ground below, and his shadow also cast rainbow colors everywhere. The cheers grew even louder as men, women, and children came out of the houses to see what all the ruckus was about.

Grinning through her tears, Jenny raised her arms upward from the elbows and spread her hands out, palms up, to show the people thronged below that *she* didn't know how this was happening, either.

Morgan woke up slowly. The first thing he saw was his own colors! He was alarmed at first, but almost immediately afterward he realized that somewhere, sometime deep inside of himself, he had dreamed of himself in these soft colors. He'd thought of that only as a dream-of-color image, which he cherished.

He became aware then of the shouting below and heard the word "Dreamsaver," shouted repeatedly. He smiled as he heard it. *Gentle Jennifer is being recognized,* he thought. Then looking down, he saw their double shadows pouring colors across the landscape and its people.

The shouts began to change. The word Dreamsaver gave way to even louder shouts of "Color Bringers!" *Color Bringers,* he thought wonderingly. *Color Bringers! They mean me too! As* he realized this, the first blush he had ever experienced glowed on his creamy cheeks, visible even through his soft down. He felt the warmth of it, which made him more embarrassed than ever, though he thought, wrongly, that whatever was happening to him wouldn't be noticeable through the down on his face.

Jennifer did notice, though, and without comment she grinned to herself.

They moved beyond the crowd, rocking in their chairs above woods, meadows, and small villages. In the villages, people who had been indoors rushed out when they noticed color seeping under doors and through windows. Those already outside gathered to discuss and delight in this incredible happening.

Children looked up and waved, and Jenny and Morgan waved back as they moved on again. Jenny wondered hopefully whether the missing children had already been found. If so, she thought, it meant that she'd been no help at all in the search for all the gone. But if the lost children had been found, she certainly couldn't be sorry. It would be a glorious finding! They went over once-white woods and forests that ignited with color as they passed. Jennifer guessed it must be autumn on the White World although there were patches of spring and summer, too. She'd never before really thought about seasons there.

A narrow road lay a short distance before them. Jenny and Morgan saw on the road a group of five Ghanglers as they became caught up in the colors. Morgan and Jenny were too high to hear what the Ghanglers said, but they saw that four of them were agitated and angry when they saw their own robes had turned to dingy grays and browns. The fifth one, the last in line, was obviously pleased with his. His robe looked almost tie-dyed, in glorious colors. He was the only Ghangler who looked up and waved at the two who were passing above.

They passed over even more trees and forest, where strange birds flew as close to them as they dared, curious about this heavenly invasion. Jennifer wished Atta Girl was with them. Maybe her cat could have understood what the startled birds were saying.

As they cut across a narrow river, a bird with a squirming fish in its mouth flew over them. When it looked down at them, its beak opened in astonishment, and the fish flopped into Jenny's lap, flipped itself right out again, fell back into the river, and swam away. Beyond the taller forest trees that lay beyond them, Jennifer recognized the clearing outside Nitty Gritty's cave door. Excitement began to build in her as she anticipated what would happen next, even though she still wasn't quite sure what had already happened.

"What was that awful place where we were, Morgan?" she asked.

"I am indubitably in doubt gentle Jennifer," he answered reluctantly. "However, some of the companions in the campground were muttering about 'the Dread,' and Nitty apparently asserted, and providentially proved, that the ancient Dread Dimension and the two chrystals were cataclysmically connected with whatever it was."

"Well, I touched the big chrystal at the bottom of the hole, Morgan, and right away I began to drift into 'the Dread,' but how did you get there?"

"When the gruesome Ghanglers grabbed me on my wandering way to Nitty Gritty's grotto I saw that, on the horribly heavy wagon they had me attempting to pull, was the crystal I'd seen in the half of the Chrystal Gate that Nitty planned to use to bring the three of thee here for a visit. I knew it was not theirs, so when I fortunately found a moment to snatch it from them, I did so."

"But …"

"I cannot conscientiously do more than guess what happened after that, when I snatched the chrystal from the sledge. I readily realized that the grim Ghanglers could no longer see me, and that I was rapidly drifting away into the weightless atmosphere. I held on to that remarkable chrystal until I was far from that place where I was so casually captured. It was not until I was over the Wandering Waters that I realized I had no idea how to bring myself down again, and I began to fear that I was dangerously doomed to invisibly orbit this planet … forever.

"With this threatening thought, I dropped the chrystal and prepared myself to fall into the treetops below"

"Hmmm," Jennifer pondered, "I guess when you dropped it, the chrystal must have made the hole I fell into, Morgan. And when I touched it, I became invisible too.

Another thing I wonder is … will the colors keep spreading and stay on the White World?"

"I devoutly desire that they will, Jennifer. Only time will tell us truly."

There was more that Jenny wanted to understand, but they were nearing the clearing now, and the biggest question then was how they were supposed to land these things!?

Chapter 22

How to Land a Rocking Chair

To cross lower sections of the mountain range, the chairs had risen higher than they'd been for the first part of the trip. Jenny was about to ask Morgan if *he* knew how they were supposed to land a couple of airborne rocking chairs, but as she turned toward him she realized that they they were already slowly descending toward the clearing. Morgan seemed unworried, so Jenny relaxed her grip on the armrests and took a deep, relieved breath.

But when she turned to look ahead again, she quit breathing altogether, and her hands gripped the armrests so hard that her knuckles were white again. They were moving more and more slowly as they descended, but not slowly enough. Although she saw someone moving around on the ground, she was much too high to tell who it might be.

Even at this slower speed, she could tell their rocking chairs were on a crash course with the side of the mountain, about ten stories above the clearing. It was true that was pretty low in comparison to the massive mountain itself, but it was way too far for them to jump before they'd crash.

Even so, she tried to untie the scarf Nitty had tied her in with, but it wouldn't budge. Morgan was trying his too, but had no more luck than she was having.

Oh, Nitty, she thought, *you're so clever about everything. However could you have made such a horrible mistake?*

With no way to save herself, Jennifer was too terrified to look. She closed her eyes tightly, her frightened tears leaking through her lashes.

She worried too that Nitty and even Behrrn might not only be shocked and saddened when they learned about the crash, but even feel guilty about it, especially Nitty. There was nothing she could do about that now, though, so her mind turned toward home. She thought about her mom's smile whenever Jenny came into the room and about Dad, teasing her as he called her "Funnyface," while treating her more like a princess.

These memories were different from the stage-set memories of the Dread Dimension. These were real memories, and they came with a twist in her heart.

She recalled teaching Warren to swim last summer. In only a couple of weeks he was a better swimmer than she was. She was so proud of him!

"Gentle Jennifer, look ahead!"

She frowned slightly as she forced her eyes open. *What was Morgan thinking?* She already knew where they were headed, did she need to watch it happen? When her eyes opened, though, she realized that they *weren't* headed for the mountain anymore. The mountain was on their left, now, and their flying chairs were very slowly, very gently, circling to their right.

"What happened, Morgan? Did you figure out how to steer these things? Or did Nitty send one of her notes with instructions? What do we do now?"

"No, there was no Nitty note, and I was not suddenly struck with inspiration. But it does seem that we are duly descending as we circle, slowly."

"Oh!" Jenny struck the side of her head with the heel of her hand. "Of course! I've watched airplanes circle the airport before landing. Why didn't I think of that?"

"No need, Jennifer. Nitty Gritty herself knew the need, and arranged it for us."

"Like a computerized program?"

"I do not know that wondrous phrase, Jennifer. But I undoubtedly do know we'll be landing soon."

"Whee-hoo!" Jenny let out her breath in a great whoosh. "Morgan dear, I don't know if my heart could have survived even one more close call."

"I fully feel with you, gentle Jennifer. Of course it wasn't at all close to catastrophe. Nitty Newfangler had things fully figured out, and she surely meant to tell us how things would happily happen. It's just that we fell asleep before she could do so."

There was no one in the landing now, but they would be down there, hopefully in exactly the right spot, in only a few more minutes. As they were coming in for a smooth and comfortable landing, Jenny found that she still couldn't undo the scarves that tied her in. Morgan tried his too but had no more success than she did.

Where was their welcoming committee? Maybe Nitty's note hadn't reached Behrrn? Maybe he was too busy to come. As Chrystellea's Rememberer, he had lots and lots of responsibilities. But he would have sent someone … wouldn't he?

They touched the ground softly, the automatic rocking chairs slowed to a stop, and the "safety scarves" slid loose on their own, falling to their sides.

Jenny and Morgan stood up on still-wobbly legs. Someone was opening the door to Nitty's cave, from the inside.

✻   ✻   ✻

When Willa looked through the small peephole in Nitty Gritty's cave door she saw part of one rocking chair on the ground, but couldn't be sure they had both landed. She didn't want to be in the way of their safe landing.

She opened the door then, just far enough to see that both chairs were down at last and that one of them held her very best friend. She threw the door open the rest of the way and rushed out to hug Jenny and then laughed as she steadied her friend. She had nearly knocked Jenny over with her enthusiasm. It was Morgan's turn next, but he was prepared for her with a big, warm hug of his own.

"However did you fly those things?" Willa demanded. "Where have you been? How come *neither* of you is white? When ..."

"Ahem." The soft cough was a gentle reminder to Willa from a woman who'd walked out behind her. She was a small woman, even for a White Worlder. Her hair was drawn severely into a tight bun on top of her head, but curls had worked their way out above her ears and at her neckline. She wore a long, straight-cut smock and a stethoscope around her neck. "These travelers have come a longer way than we can guess," she told Willa, "and they need food and rest, *now*."

"Oh yeah," Willa said with an embarrassed grin and made the introductions. "Both of you, this is Dr. Jahnn Wehlbean. Behrrn sent her with me to meet you. He wanted her to check you both out and see that you were fed and rested before he greets you. Your health was his first concern. He'll meet you tomorrow, in Chrystellea."

Jenny smiled at the doctor and at Willa, who was usually the one who remembered her manners. "I'm happy to meet you, Doctor Wehlbean," she said, not quite swallowing a yawn. "I don't know about Morgan, but I'm just fine."

"Call me Jahnn," the doctor urged. "If I'm to help you, it's probably important that you know I'm a doctor, but it certainly isn't necessary for you to repeat it whenever you speak to me." With a subtle movement, she was already taking Jennifer's pulse. "You're right that you're doing well, but you *are* exhausted."

Dr. Jahnn gasped then, staring at her own hand that had just taken Jenny's pulse. Her ivory white skin was melting into a warm, creamy chocolate, and her smock was suddenly a glowing, vivid pink.

"Wha ... what is happening to me?"

"You're absorbing the gorgeous colors that Jennifer and Morgan brought with them," Willa told her with a wide grin.

"And you look fabulous," Jennifer assured her. "Besides, that hot pink smock is just right for you. I've heard it said that pink is a color of healing. What could be better for a doctor? And your hair is the most beautiful color I've *ever* seen." The doctor's hair was the rich color of ripe peaches, with golden highlights where light touched the small curls that escaped her bun …

Dr. Jahnn coughed with embarrassment and then briskly shooed them all into Nitty's cave. She used the stethoscope to listen to their hearts and lungs and she felt their foreheads for signs of fever.

Jenny looked over at Morgan and reached for his slender hand. Even she could see how tired Morgan was. His usually perky down was drooping. It was reassuring, though, to see that the bare spaces in it were filling in again and that no more fluff was flying. But he was obviously extremely tired, so she held his hand as they followed Willa and Dr. Jaahn inside. Once there, she melted into one of Nitty's wonderful, marshmallow-soft easy chairs, while Morgan slumped into another.

Willa got busy preparing a light supper of bleggaroot broth and rippleseed rolls. She'd been taking cooking lessons while waiting for Jenny and Morgan to arrive. She served the two of them on trays where they sat, while she and Dr. Jaahn sat at Nitty's small, round table for supper. Willa was still full of questions, but she saved them for later, realizing that, as Dr. Jahnn had said, Jenny and Morgan needed food and rest before anything else.

After supper Jaahn announced that she had some house calls to make in a nearby town. "Willa will stay here with you tonight," she told the travelers briskly. "I'll come back in the morning. I won't be early, because you will no doubt be sleeping late. I'll go with you down into Chrystellea. *Please*, don't go anywhere until I return."

When Dr. Jahnn went on her way to her village calls Jenny and Morgan stood briefly while Willa went to the levers on one of Nitty's walls, the ones that put the chairs away behind domed doors, and then to the ones that called the feather-soft beds out of their own little "garages" where Nitty kept them when not in use. When they were all in cozy beds Morgan fell asleep immediately, while Jennifer settled in comfortably, figuring that she and Willa would probably talk all night with so much to catch up on.

"How did you get here, Willa," she said, rubbing sleep sand from her eyes. "How did you know how to find me?"

"Well, my dad had business in Northern California. Mom and I finagled a trip up with him so that she could visit her old friends and I could visit you. It's been *so* long! Anyway, when we learned that you and Atta Girl were missing, I just headed for the lilac bush, and ..."

Before Willa could finish her explanation, though, Jennifer was asleep again.

Chapter 23

◆

Oh, Morgan!

Before the group was halfway down the floating stepping-stone pathway to the underground realm of Chrystellea, Jennifer was grateful for the lovely night's sleep in Nitty's cave. Without that, she'd have given out well before they'd reached this point on the stairsteps, and there definitely was no good place to rest along the way.

As they descended, Jenny smiled at Jaahn's excited report about the trip she'd made to the nearby village the evening before while making her calls.

"As I moved toward the village," she told them, "color moved in front of me. The woods turned wonderful reds, oranges, and golds …" She hesitated as she described the scene, calling hopefully on her "dream of color" memories to name them. "As I came into the town, colors reached out to the people, and they were awestruck, and when …"

Dr. Jaahn's words triggered a fragmentary memory for Jennifer, of a dream she'd had the night before. When she focused on the tail end of the dream, the entire sequence spread out in her mind. In it, she was sitting on the very top of a tall, white mountain. The fields, villages, rocks, and streams that she could see were as white as the mountain. The sky, though, was as blue as a summer lake, and clouds were moving across it in slow motion like a TV commercial for insurance or perfume or something. And cutting through that sky was the clearest, brightest, most remarkable rainbow she'd ever seen. After a few moments of breathless awe, the rainbow began to separate into multicolors of butterflies—hot pink, lemon yellow, lime green, aquamarine blue, and more, with black and white, of course, to spark the colors.

Gradually, the butterflies began to settle into the all-white landscape below, and wherever they lit, colors spread out gloriously, finding where they belonged and staying there.

It was Dr. Jaahn's experiences in the village that had given her that dream, and she knew that she would never forget it again. It would be one of the first entries in the journal she planned to start as soon as ... as soon as she got home.

As Jenny, Willa, Morgan, and Dr. Jaahn continued down the stairs, they noticed that several people had gathered at the foot of the stepping-stone pathway they were descending on to the largest island, and more were coming. Jenny thought she recognized Ildirmyrth the Weaver and Prime Minister Nakeesha among them, but until she got lower, she couldn't be sure. What she could see, though, was the sparklingly clear ocean that filled the cavern below them and the few smaller islands that seemed to have been dolloped onto it. As hers and Morgan's shadows were cast over the water around the islands, it began to swirl in deep, deep blues and gleaming greens; color streamed toward the island—the capitol of Chrystellea. People were gathering at a pier. Echoes of excited voices reached Jenny and Morgan faintly, as more people gathered, hurrying and even running toward the pier.

At first the children on the ground held back, unsure of what was happening. Then a bold boy put his foot into the color that was seeping toward him. He pulled his foot back quickly, like someone testing icy water before jumping in; but that touch of the toe was enough, and color slipped instantly from his toe to the top of his head. He was startled at first, but when he took in the lovely lavender tinge of his skin, his trendy burnt-orange pants, and his acid-green shirt, he spun around with excitement, stirring his just-turned-violet hair into a shaggy purple tornado.

Other children eagerly followed his example, and they all turned themselves into delightedly twirling tops, color flowing from their hair and their fingertips, flinging streaks of grays, whites, and assorted bright, glittering colors over the walls and the underside of the enormous cavern, until the children fell, dizzy and happy onto green grass, yellow buttercups, and white-flowered clover. As the colors seeped or were flung over everything, the hues settled just where they belonged, and the process transformed the surroundings. Soon the entire cavern glimmered with flashing bits of color against varying shades of gray.

As they climbed on down watching the fun, Jennifer was able to see that it was, indeed, Nakeesha and Ildirmyrth who were waiting for them, plus a few other people she couldn't recognize from where she was. The first people to arrive had moved from the pier to the large bottom stair, so that the excited citizens wouldn't accidentally push them off the pier. Jenny was more eager than ever to get down to them. Her legs slowed her down, though. They were weak and wobbly from the long descent, and from not using them for so long while she was drifting in that weird place. What was it that Nitty had said just as she, Jenny, fell asleep? She clung to the newly installed lighted railing, though, and continued descending. She was determined to keep going.

Below, the majority of the crowd was scattering across the shores of the island, spreading colors like joy in all the happy places. Nakeesha and the few others with her were beginning to climb up the stepping-stones-in-air toward them.

Jenny looked back to smile with Willa and Morgan, but Morgan was lagging behind, his fluff drooping more than ever. His expression was resolute but desperate. Dr. Jaahn looked from where she'd been walking by Morgan's side and called the group to a halt. Morgan shakily stepped toward one of the larger stones, and Willa and Jenny both reached out to steady him as he collapsed, fainting on that stone. Dr. Jaahn was already there, and the girls settled on their own separate stones to watch while the exhausted Wohtt was being tended to.

Jenny was more grateful than ever for the handrail. She held onto it while she eased herself down. And she carefully kept her eyes straight ahead. She was *so* afraid that she might simply fall off, as she'd done on her first visit, when she'd barely escaped sudden, certain death.

Of course, Jenny realized. *Morgan was lost in that Dreadful Dimension much longer than I was. No wonder he's so tired. Oh, he's got to be all right! But how can Dr. Jaahn help him up here on these step-stones?*

She was aware that Nakeesha and Ildirmyrth were on their way up, but her attention was still on Morgan. He looked almost as white as he'd been before color came to his world, and he hadn't moved or opened his eyes since he'd fainted on the stone. Jenny approved of Dr. Jaahn, who pulled a roll of bandages out of her doctor bag. She secured the unconscious Wohtt into place, tying him to stone and railing so that no sudden movement, as he revived, would plunge him over the edge. Some wet towels were next out of the bag. They were stored in a moisture-proof packet, and she pulled them out, one at a time, placing them on his forehead and changing them every few minutes. Then she dosed him from a bottle of swirling medicine. Using something like an eye dropper, she fed the medicine, drop by drop, into his mouth.

Little by little his color returned, and the doctor nodded with satisfaction as she monitored his pulse.

"Good job, doctor," Nakeesha said as she neared the group. "It's a good thing you were with them."

Dr. Jaahn shook her head doubtfully. "I should have realized how much his reserves had been depleted while he was in the Dread Dimension."

"How could you have, Dr. Jaahn?" Nakeesha reassured her. "To my knowledge, nobody but he and Jennifer have ever gone there and returned. Now that we know, we'll be even more careful in the future, if it should somehow happen again. But see? He's moving."

"Morgan's opening his eyes!" Willa exclaimed. "He's looking around."

"I certainly shall …" His voice faltered, and then he went on. "I certainly shall be fit as fiddles. But … just a bit more rest, please, and then you can remove the restraints, for which I am grateful. It would be difficult to truly rest, with the dire threat of falling hovering over me. I am … thoroughly … thank … you …"

But he was asleep again; this time truly sleeping, not unconscious.

The friends around him on the variously sized stepping-stones lowered their voices so as not to disturb him. Even the noise from the crowd below hushed, as the people down there became aware of a problem with their beloved Wohtt.

Jennifer watched Morgan carefully for a few minutes to be sure that he really was resting, and Dr. Jaahn held his wrist, monitoring his pulse for additional reassurance.

Jenny turned to speak to Nakeesha but was distracted by one of her companions. It was a person who'd moved up just behind the Prime Minister. He was wearing a red-and-white-striped, Dr. Seuss hat. *Dr. Seuss? Here?* As Jenny looked down, the person wearing the hat tilted his head back and grinned up at her.

"Warren? *Warren!*" Jenny's mind tripped over her tongue when she recognized her brother. "Warren, what are you … how did you … why … how did *you* get here?"

"It was simple, Sis. When I saw Willa start out our back door I followed her out to the backyard, and after a few minutes I just went through the lilac bush where I'd seen her go. Elementary. She didn't know I was there until we both wound up in the campground. When everyone left, one of the gattlerbeasts volunteered to carry us here to wait for you. Nitty had explained to it that Willa and I were your best friend and family. That gattlerbeast could have won the Kentucky Derby without even trying, even with the two of us on his back." His grin nearly split his face. "Jenny, it's a *trip*, being here at last!"

Chapter 24

Sleeping

When they reached the Dreamcastle, Jennifer thought it was at last time for that great gab fest—catching up on the news with Willa and Warren, who could tell her how her parents were doing while she was missing; gossiping with Willa and learning what she'd been up to in Southern California; getting the scoop on Doug, the guy Willa had been writing about; and visiting with Morgan about how he wound up in the Dread Dimension, what he'd seen or done there, and *how* he'd recognized her when she was totally invisible. And then she'd catch up with Behrrn and their other Chrystellean friends about everything that had happened on the White World since she, Willa, and Atta Girl had last been there.

She was also eager to learn what had been heard from Nitty, Rell, and Atta Girl, who were on their way to Chrystellea on foot. How long would it be until they would get here? All those questions crowded her tired brain, and she was hoping they'd soon get somewhere she could sit down for a while.

As soon as they were away from the crowds she started in on Warren. "Okay, Warren," she said, having decided not to call him "Little Brother" anymore, "are Mom and Dad doing all right with all the"—she stopped a moment to swallow a yawn—"worry this must be causing them? And Willa's folks, too. Oh yeah, they wouldn't have worried about her until you two left the backyard through the lilac bush."

This time the yawn refused to be swallowed, and Jenny's eyes closed for a long moment before she yanked them open again. "Where's Atta Girl?" she asked, then answered herself; "Oh yeah, she's with Nitty. They'll be here when they get here." She yawned again. "I miss Atta Girl. Maybe we can go meet them on the way."

"Not yet, Jennifer," Dr. Jaahn said firmly. "We'll take you to your room, where you'll get the rest you need. When you're *thoroughly* rested there will be time enough for conversation, and for Atta Girl."

"But we ..." Jennifer looked over at Morgan, who was leaning against Willa, asleep on his feet. Willa and Dr. Jaahn were almost carrying him, and they turned into a room off the Grand Hallway. That was always Morgan's room was when he was in Chrystellea, Dr. Jaahn told her.

Through Morgan's door, Jenny could see a couple of comfortable chairs, shelves full of books, and a microscope, before Dr. Jaahn led them all past Morgan's room and the next one, which the doctor Told Jennifer was hers. The third room was Jennifer's and Willa's! It had been built for them by the dreams of Chrystellean girls, and they'd dreamed in two wonderful, comfortable beds even while Jenny was still lost. They simply dreamed that she would be found. There were unbelievably filmy curtains around the beds in ripe peach colors, but they must have been beautiful even when they were white. On every surface were jars and jugs full of fresh flowers in rainbows of colors, and luxurious lotions and soaps, arranged like still lifes on many of those surfaces.

Jennifer could see that it was a marvelous room, but she decided she could check it out more easily while resting on the bed. She drew back the curtains and slipped inside, sinking into the feathery-soft mattress. She was slightly dazed by the delicate chrystal chandelier that hung over it. It was tossing newfound rainbows over everything, rivaling the flowers for their colors.

"Dr. Jaahn," she called as the doctor started to leave the room, "while we were in the air above the mountains, I think I saw a couple of Ghanglers—dragging—children ..." Her voice faded out, and then she whispered, "Atta Girl, where are you?" But if Atta Girl had mind-sent an answer, it was too late. Jenny was already deeply asleep. Dimension traveling was overwhelmingly exhausting, probably because it hadn't allowed for *any* resting or even any awareness of tiredness along the way.

Behrrn had been hurrying toward the door to greet the travelers, and he heard what Jennifer said about the lost children. He waited outside the girls' room for Dr. Jaahn to come out and tell him more about it.

"There wasn't any more, Rememberer," Dr. Jaahn told him regretfully. "Jennifer dropped off to sleep immediately, pretty much in the middle of a sentence. "It's obvious that the trauma of her time in the Dread Dimension was serious. Neither Jenny nor Morgan should be disturbed now for *any* reason."

"But the lost children ..." Behrrn protested.

"What Jennifer knows may or may not be valuable," Dr. Jaahn told the Rememberer firmly. "But what we *do* know is that rest is all the help we can offer these two, now. As their doctor, I forbid anyone, even you, to disturb them! When she's ready, Jennifer will fill you in on what she knows, and you can decide if it will help you find the children. That is, if she actually knows anything about them or if she was already into a dream."

With that, she entered her own next door room and firmly shut the door, which was between the other two.

Behrrn and Warren walked away, slowly.

Warren had been staying in the tree house, and he couldn't get enough of exploring it, with new things coming into view all the time. No matter how much he explored in it, there was always more: more rooms—even one that looked a lot like the bridge of a spaceship, more puzzles—like a walk-through maze that was different every time he came back to it, and even the super cool, almost-parrot named Marvin, who sat on his shoulder and guided him around the place. But Marvin kept asking him when his sister, Jennifer, would get there. At first Warren hadn't known when, and even now that she was back and sleeping he was more worried about his sister than about a parrot, even one who talked like a pirate.

He turned up again at Jenny and Willa's room soon after they'd settled in. Willa insisted on staying with Jenny twenty-four hours a day until she woke up on her own. She cracked open the door and told him in whispers that the doctor said Jenny wasn't to be disturbed. Then she opened the door a bit more and told him he could tiptoe in for a minute, just to be sure Jenny was alright.

After that, he returned frequently, looked at his sleeping sister, and left quietly, only to return again, a short time later.

Dr. Jaahn put a sign on Jenny's and Morgan's doors:

NO VISITORS WHATEVER
Except for Family

Chapter 25

Clue

Willa passed the hours in one of the comfortable easy chairs, reading books she'd found on the crowded bookshelves. She couldn't concentrate on them, though. She couldn't help worrying.

One thing that kept Willa from being overcome by worry was that Lehna, the young woman that Behrrn had originally asked to help Jennifer prepare for her search, to come again and wait with Willa; they both prayed that Jennifer and Morgan would fully recover.

It wasn't until three days later, late in the morning, that Willa looked up and realized that Jennifer was finally stirring and stretching in her bed. She whispered the news to Lehna, who was dozing in the other easy chair. Even while they'd taken turns sleeping, they'd both waited anxiously for Jennifer to wake up completely. They knew that if either of them tried to hurry the process in any way, they'd have Dr. Jaahn to answer to.

Jenny woke up slowly, wondering where she was and how she got there. She raised her arm to examine the satiny, butter-yellow gown she wore. She touched the soft apple-green spread on the bed, with glints of gold in it.

She gazed at the chandelier above her. Even though it was morning, the chandelier candles glowed and dripped with chrystals. It tossed dancing rainbows on everything she could see, and as she watched, tiny rainbow-colored birds erupted from it, singing welcomes to the day before they flew out of a window that Willa would have sworn hadn't been open before. Briefly, Jenny rejoiced with them, but, as lovely as these birds were, she sort of missed Marvin, the book-loving parrot from the tree house.

Shaking her head to clear it, she reached out to touch the filmy curtain that surrounded the bed.

"Hi, Willa," she said in a hoarse, unpracticed voice. "Where are we, anyway?"

As Willa hurried to Jenny's bedside, Lehna cracked open the door and said to someone just outside, "She's awake." Then she went to Jenny's side as well, and tied the bed curtains out of the way.

Jenny sat up and put her legs over the side of the high bed, and with a smiling word from Willa, a sturdy-looking glass footstool walked over to the bedside like a pudgy puppy, then stood in position to help Jenny get down.

Laughing as she put her foot gently on the willing footstool's back, Jenny asked, "How far is it from here to the nearest bathroom, Willa?"

Willa cocked her thumb in the direction of a recessed door inside the bedroom, to which Jennifer headed as soon as her legs remembered what they were for. She called over her shoulder, "And after that, what do I have to do to get some lunch around here?"

"Lunch is on its way for us all, now that I let them know you're awake, Color Bringer."

"Thank you, Lehna," Willa said.

"Yes, *really* thank you," Jenny added. "I'm so hungry I could eat a horse."

The girl turned back, a worried, puzzled look on her face. "A horse? I'll ask, but I'm not sure the cook will have that, whatever it is."

"Sorry," Jennifer giggled. "It's just a weird saying on Earth. A horse is a very large four-legged Earth animal. Nobody could really eat a whole one, even if horse meat was good eating."

It was only a few minutes before Willa let three delighted young women in. Each of them was carrying a tray containing deliciously beautiful lunches under clear glass covers.

Jenny went to a marble basin and splashed cold water on her face. She felt a hundred percent awake and two hundred percent hungry.

Hesitantly, she sat in what she already thought of as Lehna's chair. One of the girls smilingly placed a tray on Jenny's lap; another gave one to Willa. Lehna crawled up onto the edge of Jenny's bed, where the third lunch was delivered to her.

Jenny and Willa both thanked the girls for their prompt service, and they blushingly thanked *them*, backing their way out of the door, so as not to lose sight of the Color Bringers a moment before they had to.

"Okay, friends, fill me in," Jenny said, after they were alone again and after she taken a few wonderful bites of her lunch. "I think I lost track somewhere along the way. How long have I been sleeping? Where are we, and how did we get here? And where's everybody else?"

"Well," Willa began, "we're in the Dreamcastle. Do you remember getting here, Jen?"

"I ... yes, I think so. You could have convinced me I was dreaming, but since you remember it too, it must be memory. This is new for me. I always knew the difference between real and dream, before. Anyway, what happened then?"

"So, Behrrn and Dr. Jaahn brought us here, to the guest rooms prepared for us when they learned from a Nitty note that Warren, Willa, you, and Morgan were on your way."

Jennifer looked all around the beautiful, fanciful room. Most of the assorted furniture looked like clear chrystal with soft velvety upholstery. The glassy parts shone with rainbow reflections. One of the chair backs was a parade of small elephants that paraded constantly—appearing and disappearing in unexplainable fashion. On another, the seat and arms were glass-like in appearance, but they molded to the comfort of the sitter and felt as soft as kittens. The footstool that had walked to the side of Jenny's bed wore curly-toed glass shoes on all four feet. There were more touches of dreamed-up furniture, but Jennifer didn't have time to focus on them all. "The girls dreamed wonderfully! They couldn't have had much notice."

"The girls of Chrystellea had been saving up dreams, just for this," Lehna told them proudly. Like our boys, our girls dream wonderfully."

"They sure do," Jenny and Willa agreed, almost in unison. Jennifer loved the gorgeous room they were in, but she knew she would always have a special place in her heart for the tree house and for its resident parrot.

"Dr. Jaahn's room is next door," Lehna told her. "And Morgan the Wohtt is in the one on the other side of her. Dr. Jaahn has been keeping close watch on both of you. As far as I know, our Wonderful, Wandering Wohtt is still sleeping deeply."

"Have you heard when Nitty the Newfangler and Atta Girl are expected to get here?" Jenny asked eagerly. "And Behrrn?"

"Yes, Nitty should be here within the hour, and the wonderful Atta Girl will be with her as well as Mahlee the Guide, who has been *so* worried about you! Behrrn will be here as soon as the meeting with the lost children's parents is over. He sends you his affection and best wishes for your quick recovery."

"The … lost … children. I think there's something I need to tell him about that. Well, I'd better get dressed if all that's happening." Jenny looked down at her silky nightgown, and then looked all around her. "Are there any *real* clothes handy?"

Willa and Lehna chuckled.

"Shall we tell her?" Willa asked, grinning, "Or just let her find them?"

Lehna giggled. She pulled her knees up under her chin and drew her arms around them. "Shall we give her three guesses?" she asked mischievously.

"No!" Jenny laughed with them. "You should give me three *wishes*. The first one, the second one and the third one will be that you two quit fooling around and tell me—quick!"

"Ooh! I'm afraid!" Willa giggled. "Don't let Jennifer Arthur hit me, Miss Lehna. I'll tell—I'll tell!" Still giggling, Willa opened up her left hand. In it were two silvery nuts, similar to walnuts in shape and size, but their texture was delicately carved in raised, flowerlike designs. Willa laid one of them on a small table next to her, and then opened the other one with a fancy gesture, saying, "Abracadabra! Behold! Jennifer Arthur's *real* clothes!"

Something tiny was puffing out of the small container. After a few moments Jenny recognized her very own jeans, sweater, underwear, socks, and shoes, but they were even too small for a Barbie doll. "What happened? I've heard about clothes shrinking in the laundry, but this is ridiculous!" While she protested, her clothes began to expand until Willa picked them up, shook them out, and put them on Jenny's bed, perfectly sized and ready to wear. Shaking her head in smiling wonder, Jenny changed into them, folding her nightgown on the bed where her other clothes had been when she had last seen them.

Lehna put the other "walnut" back in her pocket.

"Okay, I'm ready. I think I may know something that's important to Behrrn and the parents. Will you show us the way to the meeting, Lehna?"

"Of course, Jennifer Color Bringer." Lehna unfolded her legs. She was also too short for her legs to reach the floor, but she ignored the footstool and slid down, just as there was a soft knock on the door.

Willa stood closest, so she opened it.

"Nitty!" Jenny exclaimed. "Oomph!" She'd been struck in her midsection by a wildly purring missile. "Atta Girl!" Her eyes teared up happily. She hadn't realized just how *much* she'd missed Atta.

Rell was there too, and Beauregard, of course. Again, Jenny noticed how important the small white lion had become to Atta Girl. He was still white, but now the tips of his fur glowed with a bold tangerine color. It would be hard for Atta to leave him when they went home, but Jenny couldn't imagine what would happen if she were to try to pass off a miniature, tangerine lion to folks back on Earth.

Still cuddling Atta in her left arm, she leaned over to scratch behind Beauregard's ears. When she stood again Rell was in the doorway. He swept off his amazing wide-brimmed hat with his left hand, set it carefully on the floor, and took the chance to hug Jenny around her waist. He turned his head shyly sideways, but his hug was enthusiastic. Jennifer hugged him back, then went into Nitty's waiting arms. The Newfangler wrapped her love and her relief around both Jenny and her cat. Jennifer inhaled her fresh scent and her vitality. The Newfangler wore another kaftan, this one glowing with color. "I am so glad thou art well and rested," she said. "And now that both chrystals are together again, I shalt be able to restore the Chrystal Gate and send thee and Willa and Warren back to thy loving families."

"But not until the children are found, Nitty," Jenny insisted after she'd come up for air from the hug. "I also want to ask you what the Dread Dimension actually is. Besides, I think I have something important to tell Behrrn about those lost children. There's something kind of hovering in my memory, not quite where I can reach it. How can I get it to come closer, Nitty? How can I get at it?"

Smiling, Nitty told her, "I do indeed know the feeling, Dear Jennifer. But I be not truly sure of a slam dunk method of remembering, if there be one. methinks that the only thing that works for me is to push it away and think on something else. Often, then, that goofy thought just pops back out at me."

"Well, I'll try that, Nitty. But right now, maybe you can tell me if Morgan and I really were in the long lost Dread Dimension."

"That's our best guess, Jenny," Nitty said, nodding.

Well, I have lots of questions I'd like to ask later, but right now I'd better get to that meeting Behrrn's having with the parents. I'm pretty sure that what I haven't quite remembered has to do with their missing children."

From the back of the group, almost as if she'd been hiding, was Mahlee. There were tears in her eyes, and when she reached Jenny, she took both of her hands into her own. "Oh, Jennifer, I can't hardly stand the shame. I was asked t' take keer of you, but you up and got lost ennyhow. I reckon you went through some awful stuff afore Nitty got you back. I be purely ashamed!"

"Oh, Mahlee dear, there was no way you could have prevented it. There was a warning sign on the hole, and I ignored it."

"To save Little Bee," the square little guide reminded her.

"Well, the only way that could be changed was to take the chance that it would be Bee who fell in. This way was better, and you couldn't have prevented it. She was too fast for any of us, getting in there." She grinned at Mahlee, who grinned back through her tears.

"I do be grateful fer yer understandin', Jennifer."

"Come on with us to talk to Behrrn," the teenager answered as she kept hold of one of the guide's hands and started off behind Lehna again, signaling for the others to come, too. But before they'd gone only a few steps, they were interrupted.

"Jen," her brother called as he hurried their way, "you're awake! How d'you feel? Where are you going?"

"Hi, Bro!" Jenny grabbed Rell's hand and pulled him close. "Remember me telling you about my brother, Warren? Well Rell, here he is, in the living flesh!"

Grinning, Warren tipped his Dr. Seuss hat. "That's a fine-looking lid you've got there, Rell. As one hat lover to another, glad to meet you. Wait a minute—does that vine on your hat actually have *fruit* on it? Can it be actually *growing* there?"

Rell didn't answer right away. When they'd all left the campground at different times and in different directions, he'd been afraid he'd never meet his hero, Warren, again. He quickly caught on to Warren's little joke and went right into it, pretending he and Warren had never before met. He nodded. "Yes, it's growing," he said. "It only has a little fruit on it right now, though. I guess I've been doing a lot of snacking on it on the way here. But Great Galaxies! That hat of *yours* is the most amazing topper I've ever seen."

While they were talking, Jennifer noticed a grandmotherly lady sitting in a rocking chair in a nearby hall alcove. The tiny woman had been knitting something with subtly colored yarns, which seemed to be softly lit from within. Now, though, she was watching the "meeting" of the two boys with a glad smile.

"I guess you must be the person who's been watching out for us and taking care of messages when they were needed," Jennifer said to her. "And I do thank you, *so* much!"

"You are abundantly welcome, Color Bringer," she replied in a surprisingly young voice. "But I'm only one of three who've been taking eight-hour shifts. We're all grateful for the privilege of serving you, in gratitude for the wonders you have brought to our formerly pale planet."

"Well," Jennifer admitted, "I'm not really sure how it all happened. It was really kind of an accident. I only hope it lasts!"

"It will last," the woman serenely assured her. "It has your touch in it."

As the group moved on, they passed Morgan's door. She sent the still-sleeping Wohtt a prayer. Surely he would wake up very soon too!

Warren and Rell were yakking away like old friends, and she was pleased for both of them.

They passed through exquisite halls and rooms on their way to the meeting hall. Besides being gorgeous, they were all fantastically unique rooms or areas in one way or another. There was so much to see that Jenny was able to do a fair job of focusing on the surroundings instead of on her elusive memory.

There was the room with an indoor pool, which seemed more like a small river. It began at a far wall where water cascaded down with a satisfying roar. Shallow falls sang between levels until they finally slipped under another wall, this one clear as glass, to hum along merrily out of sight. There weren't a lot of swimmers, but there appeared to be many different species there and even—Jenny thought she must be mistaken—a trio of mermaids, who were combing their long, sea-green hair while sitting on one of the huge rocks that bordered the pool.

Then there were the wide halls, with trees bursting from the walls near the arched ceilings high above them. The branches dripped with something like Spanish moss, though it was translucent and quivered with silvery light.

They passed wide, double doors that opened into the Walk/Run Room—a huge space with complicated, twisting, earthen paths. Some paths were flat while others were hilly, to varying degrees. They were arranged so that the walker or runner could go from one level to another, and another and another, yet stay consistently on a single level. Even though she moved by the room quickly, Jenny glimpsed a climbing wall on the room's far side, which was very far up indeed.

But the most fascinating part was the creatures who were walking and running there. Along with Chrystelleans as she knew them, there were … then suddenly Jenny's elusive memory plopped, fully developed, into her brain. Oh, she *had* to get to Behrrn as soon as possible. She hoped that it would be wonderfully important information for those parents whose children were lost.

Until they reached the meeting room, Jennifer didn't notice any more of the wonders they passed by. All she thought about was the children and what she'd seen—or hoped she'd seen.

When they got there, Lehna went into the meeting hall and came out with Behrrn, who went directly to Jenny. He put both of his big hands on her small ones.

"Is it possible, Jennifer Arthur, that after all you have *already* accomplished for our world, you well may now lead us to our lost children? What a generous miracle you are!"

"I'm not a miracle, Rememberer." Jenny felt her face heat up, and she wondered if Behrrn had had enough experience with color by now to recognize a blush. She hoped not. "Bringing the color was more of an accident. It's as if the color trapped in the Dread Dimension recognized the color in me, and sort of glommed onto it and pulled. It was just lucky that I was able, with Morgan's help, to get out of there at all and to bring color along with us.

"Anyway, I'm not *sure* I saw anything to help at all, but when Morgan and I were flying along in Nitty's rocking chairs, the colors were just then in the process of pouring onto the white mountains. The changing colors made it hard to make details out clearly, so it's hard to know for sure, but it seemed like there was a high meadow nested between three mountains. As the color edged into it, I saw that it was grassy, and there were some shrubs and at least one tree. So there must have been plenty of soil there, not just rock."

"Ghanglers are rarely seen traveling through mountains," Behrrn said regretfully. "But of course we don't *know* who the kidnappers are. We will check out that site as soon as possible."

"There's more, Behrrn, although this is the part that the changing colors made so very hard to make out. Anyway, I think—I'm *pretty sure* that I saw a Ghangler walking across the field, and he had hold of two small children by the hands. And as color started to crawl up the side of the mountain where he was headed, a huge black area showed that there was a cave there, and the Ghangler was *dragging* the children toward it."

There was a collective gasp of surprise and horror from all those within earshot. Behrrn was the first with an action response.

"Jennifer, this is the most hopeful news we've had since children began disappearing! I must tell the parents and dismiss the meeting. Then we shall set up a group to explore this possibility!"

"The group will have to include me," Jenny said firmly. "I couldn't tell you how to get there. I'd have to fly in the rocking chair again to locate it."

"So be it," Behrrn answered with a resolute look. He quickly returned to the meeting room to deliver hopeful news to the grieving families.

Chapter 26

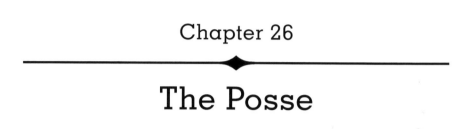

The Posse

Choosing the search party was pretty easy. There would be Nitty, of course. She located two additional rockers, which would help a lot. Then Jenny, because she was the only one who could find the high meadow again, (she hoped). Atta Girl would go with Jenny in her chair, and Beauregard the lion would go with Atta. Mahlee Kahdell also insisted almost tearfully that she be included. She felt she could never work as a guide again if she were not allowed to be included in this potentially dangerous expedition.

Rell hopped up and down with his hand in the air to volunteer. Behrrn considered him gravely. "I am sorry, Rell, but your parents have not arrived here yet. At your age, we would have to have their permission."

Poor Rell slumped, with his hands pushed deep into his pockets. He knew that even if his mom and dad had been there, they'd never let him go.

Then Warren stepped forward to volunteer.

"How old is your brother, Jennifer?" Behrrn asked as he smiled at Warren.

Jenny glanced at her eleven-year-old brother, who stared back at her challengingly. "He's—he's thirteen," she lied, "almost fourteen. He could be a lot of help."

"Fine," Behrrn said with a small grin. He'd seen through Jenny's lie, but Warren seemed mature enough to be a help, anyway.

"Get a good night's sleep," he told the group. Jenny winced as she thought about even more sleeping time. "We'll meet in the morning at Nitty Newfangler's place. Is that alright with you, Newfangler?"

"Surely 'tis, but mayhap 'twould be even more of a zinger if we all simply slumber at my place. We couldst achieve an earlier start, in that manner."

"Great!" Behrrn agreed. "All of you bring along whatever might help us with you, as long as it's easy to carry. I'll tie up some loose ends down here, then I'll be the group's alarm clock in the morning."

True to his word, only the palest of the White World's suns had cleared the horizon when he knocked and came through the corner cupboard into Nitty's cave. The posse, as Warren had dubbed the group, had risen even earlier. They were ready and had already had a hearty breakfast.

They all went to the clearing outside Nitty's front door where, before jumping into two of them, Behrrn and Warren set the four rocking chairs in motion. Jennifer, Nitty, Willa, and Warren were assigned as the Rocker Guiders. Atta Girl took over Jenny's lap, and Warren welcomed Beauregard onto the one he shared with Mahlee. They all tied themselves into their respective chairs with the security scarves. With a stern admonition, Behrrn told the posse to "wait for me," because he had decided to try walking through the power circle tunnel that had appeared there some weeks ago. He felt sure it led, and was probably even a shortcut, to the same place that the others were headed, and he would join them there.

Then with a signal from Nitty Gritty, the rocking chairs began to rise until their passengers were airborne. When Nitty felt they were high enough, the chairs slowly began to move in the direction Jenny indicated.

It might be a tougher job to find the place from this other side, Jenny realized. Although she was more awake than she had been last time, things just looked so *different* from this direction.

She grew more and more stressed as they skirted along part of a small mountain range on the way to Too Tall Mountain. When they went beyond that mountain, her heart began to beat faster as she looked so hard, she felt as if her eyes might drop right out. Even so, they had almost passed right by the meadow she'd seen before when Warren called, "Hey Sis, is that the place you described?"

Nitty turned all the rockers around, and Warren was right. It was *exactly* the place.

The rockers hovered for a few minutes as Behrrn caught up with them through the power circle, and then they landed at the opposite end of the meadow from the cavern entrance and disembarked. Nitty stayed in one of the rockers and took Warren's now-empty chair. Holding it by one of its arms she floated to the ground where Behrrn waited.

When Nitty and the Rememberer rejoined the group they gathered in the high meadow, where Warren spotted a nearby power circle. It was an empty one, Jenny thought gratefully. It was outlined in stiff, cutout-looking sunflowers, although these had purple petals and red centers, instead of yellow.

Behrrn noted it too, then looked ahead to study the grassy area that dominated the meadow. He stooped and traced his finger above, but without touching, some spiraling patterns in the grass. "Whirly prints," he told them grimly.

The tracks led directly to the huge cavern entrance that Jenny had told them about.

"But what about these marks that come out sometimes on the sides of the whirlyprint trail?" Warren asked.

"Children's feet," Behrrn almost snarled, "Children being *dragged*." He set out directly across the meadow in strides so long that the others had to jog to keep up.

Behrrn was furious! Jenny had never even seen him even cross before, and judging by the startled looks from Nitty and Mahlee, she guessed they never had either. Jennifer's eyes stung with tears, but she shook them out of her eyes impatiently. *We're coming, kids,* she thought. *I don't know what we'll do when we get there, but we'll do something. We're coming!*

Chapter 27

Deep Within

Far below the room at the cavern's entrance was another even more enormous cave room thick with white mists. Feeling their way through that eerie fog, dozens and dozens of children labored at various jobs. The exhausted older children were busy chipping away rock in several places. Their job was to create room-sized extensions to the enormous main room. Visible on one side were glimpses of already inhabited "apartments," comfortably furnished for the wind-walking Ghanglers.

The younger children, hardly more than toddlers themselves, took care of the babies. The babies were bedded down on beds of straw, covered with scraps of dirty fabric. The children caring for them fed them with rags dipped in pans of a milky liquid and tried to keep them from crying. Crying could be dangerous for the babes and for their small caretakers, as well.

Near the center of the activity, in a small, highly visible area, was the whirlwind-walker who was even taller than the rest of the Ghanglers. And meaner. The Ghanglers surrounding him cleared the mists around him with fans and blow-tubes. Tehran Tuhlla the Absolute was speaking to his followers.

"Fellow Ghanglers," he ranted, "look around you and see the beginnings of a new and color-free city for us and for our small companions." He sweepingly gestured toward the children with a dreadful sneer. The "companions" never lifted their heads. To stop working even for a moment was also perilous.

"Those of us who have left this area for supplies, bring us terrible news!" he continued. "The monstrous colors I have repeatedly warned you about are *spreading across our own White World!*"

A scandalized, even frightened murmur rose from the crowd.

"But do not fear!" Tuhlla screeched in triumph. "They will not dare to enter this, our refuge and our fortress. We shall rule the planet from here, and none will risk hindering our emissaries from their tasks, which shall be to keep this city-to-be supplied and comfortable. As long as we have their children, they will not oppose us. And we will raise these children to loyally serve us, and *only* us."

The mists suddenly overcame the fan-wavers and blowers, blotting out Tehrran Tuhlla's message as it *should* have been. Except for the children's areas, the murmurs quickly changed to ragged cheers. Delaying Tehran's applause was also dangerous, even for Ghanglers.

Chapter 28

◆

Unexpected Menace

As the posse moved cautiously into a second cavern, color moved in slowly with them. Colors had stopped spreading at the entrance of the cavern since no suns reached there to throw their colorful shadows ahead. Some muted color did, though, move in closely with the searchers, flowing from them. Darkness cut through the mists here, but some light from outside the tunnel created a subtle reflection gleaming from the rock walls. It helped lead the way for the rescue group.

There was no sign of anyone there, except for the chittering clatter of some rat like creatures whose hot yellow eyes watched the group from the darkest niches.

"Those are sluggyucks," Behrrn told the others. "They're slimy and evil-looking, but they don't attack living things."

That reassured the group somewhat, but when they caught clearer glimpses of them, they saw that their teeth were long and sharp-looking. They were curved inward too—the better to tear apart their food. Jenny shuddered. Their claws clattered on the rocks, setting up a constant, distant-sounding din.

☆   ☆   ☆

Things had been fairly quiet for a while in Tuhlla's underground city. Only an occasional cry from one of the babies and the quick shushing of their caretakers broke the monotonous sounds of the older children, fighting against exhaustion as they continued chipping away at the rock.

Tehrran Tuhlla the Absolute was lounging on a stone easy chair that had been chipped out by the children under close supervision, and then thickly padded for his comfort. Suddenly he leaped up, screaming with fury. "Colors! Vile colors have moved into the cavern entrance! They must not reach us here!

"Counselors! Recommendations for defense … *now!*"

His closest companions moved stealthily away from him, crowding behind each other to escape his notice. Even his personal whirlwind, which was almost flattened out on the rock floor, slid slyly away, plumping up and nervously twitching as it moved.

"*You!*" Tuhlla's clawlike index finger pointed directly at one of the discreetly retreating Ghanglers. "What advice have you to give for fighting this menace?"

"Sire," the shrinking Ghangler said, coughing with nervousness. "There has never, in any recorded history, been an attempt by any people or rulers to conquer us Ghanglers."

"Enough!" Tuhlla's whirlwind sparked and lashed out at the unfortunate adviser, who, not quite in time, skittered out of reach. Tuhlla's voice lowered threateningly. "Every problem has to be dealt with a first time. I expect all of you to gather in yon apartments and come up with a creative solution. *Now.*"

✳   ✳   ✳

At first the posse thought they'd found only another empty cave. They knew from tracks though, in the areas where there was some soil for moss to grow in, that Ghanglers had been there with the children. Then they, or some of them, had gone out again, although they saw only whirly prints going in the out direction … no children's footprints.

Warren patted the many roomy pockets on his cargo pants and pulled out two flashlights.

"Warren Arthur," his sister exclaimed admiringly, "where did you find those? I didn't think there was such a thing in the White World."

"I brought them from home, Jen. I thought Willa might be planning to head somewhere important when she went out our backdoor, so I grabbed anything in reach that might come in handy and followed her.

Everybody laughed, relieved, with Nitty's throaty laughing coming through. "Jennifer's brother," she said, chuckling, "What else might thee have tucked away in those wowee pockets, just in case?"

"Oh, a bunch of stuff, Ms. Newfangler," Warren answered. "As a matter of fact, if anyone's hungry I've got lunch in here too." Proudly, he patted his pockets again.

"Perhaps not yet," Behrrn said, after looking around the group for their responses. "But I'm sure we'll be most grateful later on. Thank you, Warren."

"Sure thing." Warren handed Behrrn one of the flashlights and kept the other, leaping suddenly sideways as he did, to avoid an especially bold skuzzyukk. Behrrn watched carefully as Warren switched his flashlight on, then switched on the one he held as well. Wonderingly, he sent its light exploring over the cavern. When the light touched one of the darkest areas, they saw another opening. Another passageway showed a tunnel entrance to, possibly, another cavern. Someone moved, accidentally kicking a loose rock. Everyone stood still, holding their breaths, until the rock rattled and rolled into a long, deep crevasse in the floor of the passageway. It was a long, long time before they faintly heard it hit bottom.

They eyed the dark opening warily, but Behrrn led the group into it with the flashlight he held showing the way. Warren got in the middle of the line, right in front of his sister. He could be sure, from there, that Jenny wouldn't stumble and fall along the way. *That*, he assured himself with satisfaction, *is what brothers are for.*

The skuzzies, as Jenny had begun to think of them, streamed back and forth along the passageway with them. Jenny and the others had to hop and leap to get by the things, as well as watch the pathway which was steeply descending. One of the skuzzies brushed Jenny's leg, and she smothered a shriek, realizing why Behrrn had called them slimy.

As they went on down and around a bend, chittering and clattering of the skuzzies grew louder. The group almost fell over each other when they stumbled into a still another clump of skuzzyukks. They were apparently fighting over something dead in the tunnel pathway. The posse members shuddered and edged around them.

When they emerged from the passage into another large, fairly level cave room, the relief was so great that an almost-electrical current flowed through them all. They'd needed that shared comfort to give them the courage to continue their hunt. And the flashlights revealed something else, which absolutely proved that Ghanglers had been there. On a low ledge they saw something sparkling like oversized, energetic fireflies, and when they moved closer they saw the sparkly things stir and become candy-colored, as well.

"Whirlies!" Willa exclaimed with alarm.

"Apparently," Behrrn guessed. "Ghanglers must keep a supply of spare whirlwinds on hand here in this cavern." Everyone agreed that they were whirlies, but none of them had ever seen them sparkle when Ghanglers were using them.

"Maybe the sparkles are a kind of stored energy?" Willa suggested. "And when they're in use, the sparkle energy is being used to carry Ghanglers around instead."

For want of a better explanation, everybody agreed it might be that way.

There was a more important dilemma to solve, though. Instead of one exit on the other sides of the room, there were several. Which one should they follow?

Before following any of them, Nitty Gritty produced some kind of glow-in-the-dark chalk and carefully marked the one they'd just come through.

Atta and Beauregard wandered off, sniffing out all of them.

"Excellent thinking, Newfangler," Behrrn said with an approving smile. "Now we'd best brainstorm our next move." They gathered near the whirly ledge to talk things over. Jenny, though, couldn't ignore the many passage entryways, even when she tried. Whether she was looking at them or not, they reminded her too much of her too-recent experiences with the Dread Dimension. She was glad Morgan was still resting back in the Dreamcastle. Again, Jennifer was reminded of how long *he* had endured the Dread Dimension alone. It was much longer than she had.

Someone in the group suggested leaving to get help. Jenny wanted to agree with that, but the children were here *now*. Someone else suggested exploring the passages one at a time, from left to right, numbering them with Nitty's chalk, or else … Atta's mindspeech reached each of them at the same time when she announced, *Thisss way,* pointing with one paw to the third passage from the left. *Voicesss therrre,* she added. *Ghannngler voicesss, perrrrhapssss.*

Just then, Jennifer felt an odd sensation on the calf of her leg. She'd already started screeching when she looked down to see that one of the whirlies had somehow slit a small spot in her jeans and attached itself to her skin.

Willa giggled. "It likes, you, Jenny," but it turned out not to be funny at all. Jenny tried to shake it off, and couldn't. She tried to pull it off, with no success. The thing just stuck to her hands, as well. Warren brought a pair of work gloves out of one of his pockets. Using them, he and the others all tried, but they couldn't pull it off either. Meanwhile, it was spreading, a sparkling pink membrane, stretching down to immobilize her feet, and climbing up toward her chest.

Warren found shears in one of his pockets, and tried to cut the whirly off. The best he could do was release Jenny's hands so she could stand up straight again. Then the membrane snatched the scissors out of Warren's hand and plastered them against Jennifer's knees, a frightful decoration.

Everybody, including Behrrn, tried different ways to free Jennifer, but the whirly-membrane crept almost up to her shoulders, pinning her inside it. Horror crept over her as the thing spread, and her fear was mirrored in the eyes of her friends, especially Warren's. That was his *sister* there! Without stopping to think—thinking hadn't got him anywhere!—he picked a skuzzyukk up by the tail with his work gloves on, and *threw* it at Jenny, right at the place where the whirly had first grabbed onto her. The others gasped and Jenny, who was now nearly up to her chin in whirly-stuff, asked with a sob, "Oh Warren, *why!*"

He choked on his own sobs. "I don't know, Sis. I *don't know!* I just couldn't think of anything else." He beat on both sides of his head, as if he could knock a right idea into it.

"But *look!*" It was Behrrn who first noticed what was happening. "The skuzzyukk—it's *eating* the membrane."

"And the whirly is dropping away from her," Willa screeched happily as the limp remains fell to the floor. She moved to Jenny, grabbing her in a careful hug to keep her from falling to the cave floor as she was freed. As Jennifer cautiously stepped out of it, it was immediately swallowed by as many skuzzyukks as could get at it.

"It looks like those yucky things just discovered that they like whirlies, *a lot*," Willa said with a nervous laugh.

"Well, I sure don't!" Jenny's laugh trembled too, but it *was* a laugh. She still clung to Willa for support while the blood flowed painfully back into her legs and arms. Nitty, Mahlee, and Behrrn came forward to hug her, but they had to nudge their way past Warren, who held her from behind in a superhug. He moved away, though, for Behrrn and then Nitty and Mahlee.

"Gollee, Jennifer!" the Newfangler whispered into her ear as they hugged, "coming so near to losing thee yet again, was not merely scary, 'Twas *gross! Terrifying!*"

"Thanks to my brother." Jennifer looked gratefully in Warren's direction. "I owe him my freedom and probably my life. As a matter of fact, I'd like to know what other good ideas he has."

"That wasn't a 'good idea,' sis; that was *desperation*. Anyway, the best thing I can think of now is for you to rest awhile." He rummaged through his pockets, pulling out health bars, apples, bananas, and packaged fruit drinks. "Why don't we all take time out for lunch now?"

"Well, no one can deny *that's* a great idea!" Behrrn put action to his words, using Warren's gloves to shove the remaining whirlies clear to the far side of the ledge, then onto the floor, where the skuzzyukks immediately cleaned up the mess. "Behold, ladies and gentleman," he said, gesturing toward the cleared ledge with a sweeping bow, "our lunchroom and our lunch await."

Smiling proudly, Warren passed out the goodies he'd stowed away as everyone found a place on the ledge. The girls tucked their legs under them, just in case.

Everyone finished lunch, even the homemade cookies Warren had stored in baggies. They'd all, except for Jennifer, who was still a bit queasy, finished quickly and gratefully.

"Should we try the passage that Atta Girl and Beauregard recommend?" Behrrn asked.

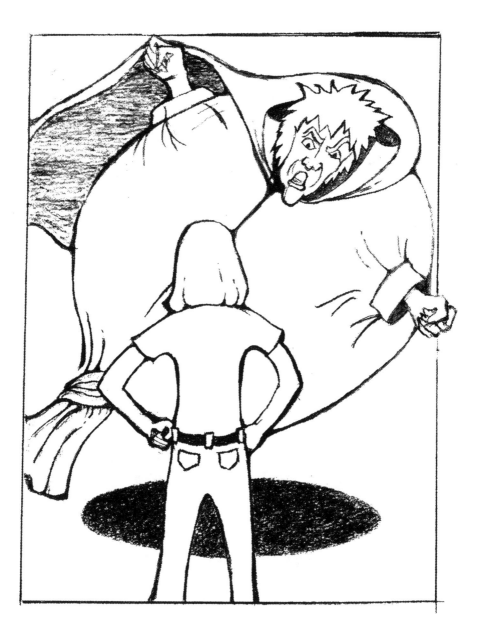

Chapter 29

◆

Blowhard

In the lowest cavern, where the Ghanglers and their kidnapped prisoners hid out, the most threatening thing that could be seen was Tehrran Tuhlla. He couldn't pace, but he slithered wildly back and forth on his whirlwind. The whirlwind didn't quite fit, since it had spread out, and had to keep pulling itself back in, as well as it could. Tehrran was mumbling furiously. His whirlwind reflected its owner's mental state by lashing out in all directions, stinging whomever it was able to reach. Its reach lengthened more and more as Tuhlla ranted. Occasionally, when Tuhlla's mumblings rose to a roar, his whirlwind actually ignited small fires in Ghanglers' robes, and even, in two or three cases, spit lightning far enough and high enough to light sparks in shaggy Ghangler hair.

Batting at the fires to try to put them out, Tuhlla's thugs moved farther and farther back, crowding against the walls and pushing children aside behind the stalagmites in their search for safety—not from the colors but from their leader.

When the posse entered Atta's recommended passageway Jennifer followed reluctantly—only because following was slightly better than staying behind, alone. More and more, these passages and rooms reminded her of the Dread Dimension tunnels, and she still wondered just what that had been. At least in these rooms and passages, she had company. Here too she could actually feel things and interact with everything, even when these things were horrifying. She reminded herself to be grateful.

As they descended the cavern more and more steeply, her knees got sore as the drop increased, but she was grateful for her marshmallow shoes. When she and her family had visited Carlsbad Caverns, her toes got terribly painful as the downward incline pressed them hard against the toes of her leather shoes. Anyway, pain was better than the nothingness of the Dread Dimension.

A horde of skuzzies followed behind them, like rats following the pied piper out of Hamelin. They didn't seem interested in getting ahead of them. They even kept a small distance between the posse and themselves. They didn't bother Jenny *too* much. But even though they had eaten off the whirly thingamawhat that had nearly swallowed her, she couldn't manage to work up a fondness for those skuzzy things, either.

Jenny moved quietly along with her friends and her brother who was also a friend—a really good friend! She could barely see the others, as color and natural darkness moved before them. The flashlights were turned off but held ready in case of an emergency. Although she couldn't see them right then, she knew that everyone in the posse was grimly determined. Their nerves, like hers, were alert and edgy.

When a sudden scream of rage echoed through the caverns, Jenny almost turned back, but then they heard the cry of a small child quickly muzzled. After that, there was absolutely no doubt about what they must do. *Okay*, she reminded herself, *so it might be smarter to go back for help. Meanwhile, though, Ghanglers are here, and so are the children.*

They moved even more quietly, scarcely breathing. The darkness was complete as they continued toward the lunatic sounds of a madman. Then, a faint light could be seen from the gigantic chamber ahead.

To avoid being seen in the tunnel where they could be easily trapped, they halted, still in the passageway. They were still silent, although it seemed unnecessary, what with the furious screaming that bounced off the stone walls. They could make out more and more of the screamed words as they got closer, words like "colors," "aliens," "cat," and "hideous."

Jennifer shuddered, but when the group began to move ahead, she kept moving with them. The cushy shoes they all wore were silent too.

When they reached the huge cave room, Behrrn signaled each of them, one by one, toward nearby stalagmites they could hide behind. They entered the enormous room one at a time, hugging the rock walls, dodging individually as Behrrn directed them into the wall's occasional niches. One by one, as they moved out of the tunnel, they were sheltered in the shadows in the various niches and behind the stalagmites that rose from the cavern floor, conveniently near its exit. From that position they were able to watch Tuhlla the Absolute scream, spit, and threaten, while they assessed the situation and tried to figure out *how* to rescue the children.

Tuhlla twisted and turned as his whirlwind tried to keep up with him. He seemed to be looking for enemies in the various muted colors that now penetrated that room, dispelling most of the white mists that had curled through it.

The Ghanglers shrank back farther and farther as Tuhlla continued to howl and roar his hate and his fear, which were, Jennifer suddenly realized, one and the same. Tuhlla was afraid of *them!*

Some of the children, looking for places to hide, slipped quietly behind stalagmites too, either not noticing or not alarmed by the posse members who were already there. When some of the frightened Ghanglers shoved their way behind stalagmites, though, some of the children were roughly pushed out. The posse members moved out of the children's way and stood together in the open, in front of the children but still in shadows.

As Tuhlla continued to twist and turn, his long robe twisted at the bottom like a wrung-out dishrag. The radius of his whirlwind widened. It spit more sparks and stretched wider and farther away from Tuhlla himself. As it disconnected itself from the head Ghangler, it seemed that only Tuhlla's fury was holding him up, inflating him like a New Year's parade float.

A bold and curious two-year-old stepped out of the designated area for the children. He came almost to Tuhlla's power circle and looked up at him in wonder.

Tuhlla bent way over to him, and roared, "Get back where you belong, brat!" At the same time, with his long, skinny arm and his clawlike hand, he knocked the toddler several feet away, against the stony, jagged cavern wall.

Well, Jenny tried to count to ten as she'd been taught, but she only got to two before *that* little episode was just too much for her. She took a long step out of the shadows, toward Tuhlla His Terribleness (one of her own names for him). "How *dare* you hit a child," she said loudly, to be heard over the child's hiccupping sobs. "You think that makes you a big shot? Well, think again, thug. All it makes you is a coward and a *blowhard*."

Tuhlla blew up even larger, so that he floated several inches above the stone floor. "The alien! She's here! They're all here and their traitorous allies as well." At that moment while she was glaring at the absurdly ballooning chief Ghangler, she felt Willa move up to stand by her left side and Warren on the other. She was aware too that all the rest of the posse was lined up beside them.

Tuhlla blew himself impossibly bigger and screamed, "Ghanglers, attack the alien invaders!" His overworked whirlwind stretched out still farther, spat out a spurt of fireworks good enough for a Fourth of July backyard celebration, then flattened out limply, with no more sparkle of any kind.

Quietly, some skuzzyukks approached and began to dine on it.

The intimidated Ghanglers, those who weren't already hiding, moved as if to obey the command. Instead of going toward the "invaders," though, with startled looks on their faces they all swayed like tenpins on the verge of a strike, and then crumpled to the rocky floor. It seemed the Ghanglers had been so focused on Tuhlla's tantrum that they hadn't noticed the skuzzies quietly nibbling at their whirlwinds. The slimy creatures were moving out of the room now, waddling slightly and licking their chops with great satisfaction. The Ghanglers sat or lay helplessly, their whirlwind "feet" having disappeared.

"ATTACK!" Tuhlla howled, infuriated at the unexpected collapse of his followers. "Attack, you fools!" At each screeching command, Tuhlla blew up even more, until with a sudden *pop!* the so-called "Absolute" deflated rapidly, spinning like a blown-up balloon when it's let loose.

He rose so high his head smacked the ceiling, and circled the cave wildly until he neared an entrance to a ceiling opening where he was sucked—or impelled—toward an upward-bound passageway. He slid away, flailing and screaming near the ceiling and closer and closer to that passage. He finally disappeared upward, sucked screaming into the hole.

There was a long moment of silence as everyone in Tuhlla's city-to-be tried to take in what had happened. The few Ghanglers who'd been hiding came out and began to toss their whirlwindless fellows over their shoulders and carry them out. The children began to stir and talk and eventually laugh, when they realized that Tuhlla was somehow gone and that those who remained were somehow harmless.

"Victory!" Warren hollered, standing with his feet apart hero style, holding a slingshot in one hand, and a stone in the other. "And *not a single shot fired.*"

Chapter 30

◆

Returning

Jenny, Warren, Nitty, Willa and the cats took the rocking chairs back to the Nitty's home/lab entrance, then scurried through her cave and down to the underground nation to let the parents know their children were safe, and that they were on their way to them. Behrrn and Mahlee traveled with the children through Bluhgg Woods to Chrystellea's other entrance.

As Jenny's group rocked their way toward Nitty's place, she answered questions that the others had been asking her concerning the Dread Dimension. Some she had answered, but there were still questions Jenny herself wanted to ask."

"Why did the Dread Dimension try to keep me there," Jenny asked Nitty, "but not Morgan?"

"Possibly it had no reason to keep Morgan," Nitty guessed. "Remember, you said it was making a wall between you, with Morgan already on the exit side. Perhaps it sensed that there was color hidden in you, and after all the eons of holding this world's colors within itself, it—or they, if there are separate entities accidentally imprisoned there—must have come to believe that its "job" was to be the White World's official Color Keepers, since that, apparently, is what it has been doing since the beginning of our time."

"I wonder what it will do now that the White World and its people have found the color that was always meant for them," Warren remarked.

"Well, everybody knows about the Dread now, so nobody else needs to be caught up in it," Jenny hoped. "I have to admit though, that some things I learned in its rooms were things I needed to learn. I don't know why they showed me those memories, but it was good for me to see them.

I haven't had a chance, yet, to ask Morgan if that happened to him too."

She hesitated a moment, her forehead puckering with worry. "He's got to be okay!"

"He'll probably be waiting for us when we get back, all ruffled because he didn't get to come with us," Nitty assured her.

Jenny was reassured, because Nitty was almost always right. "But still, Nitty, why *my* memories? Why did that Dread thing pull those out of my mind for me to look at?"

"I've been wondering about that too," Nitty Newfangler answered slowly. "Of course, I can't know for sure. But one theory might be that they weren't showing them for thee. Maybe they were showing them for themselves. Entities that may have been trapped in that dimension must be bored … and lonely! Maybe that was just their goofy way of getting to know you …"

"Getting to know me? But that's not me. I mean, it was just some things I once did or saw or thought about. It's not me *now*."

"There's absolutely no better way for others to get to know thee as thou art now, than to know how you've become who you are. It's even the absolutely best way for thyself to see fully what thoughts and experiences brought thee to here and now. That's why I keep journals; to remember the thoughts and experiences and friends who have made me who I am." She delved into a pocket in her caftan and pulled out a beautiful, flower-covered book. "Sometimes, when I am reading back in my journals, I discover things I think that I didn't really know I thought. Or that I've changed my mind about."

Jenny nodded. She used to believe that she never forgot anything that ever happened. She rested her feet on the rockers as she thought it all over, meditating about what Nitty had said. There'd been things in those memory rooms that she'd completely forgotten and some that she'd only remembered when the rooms reminded her.

She pulled her feet back and tucked them under her, the safety belt surprising her by stretching to allow her to do it. She reminded herself that there were things in some of those memories that she needed to remember. There were lessons for her there.

But there was so much to be glad about now! She felt as light as if her bones were hollow, almost as if she could fly like a bird without a rocking chair. Morgan was surely getting stronger and stronger, the missing Chrystal was back in Nitty Gritty's capable hands, and the children were *all* safe, and soon would be back with the people who loved them.

All the gone had been found, and even if Jenny hadn't truly found Morgan and the Chrystal herself, she had been there to help find and rescue the children. Even though she'd asked the posse not to talk about the part she'd played in their rescue, because she was embarrassed that she'd lost her temper again. It was pure satisfaction to her that she'd helped, anyway. *Sometimes*, she realized, *temper wasn't just temper, it was indignation!*

With the Chrystal Gate gems safely under lock and key in Chrystellea, and the very, very, very deep hole filled up before the last of the campers left the area, the Dread Dimension would have to get by without any more captive friends. Besides, now the entire White World was vibrant with brilliant colors, and Jenny, Atta Girl, Willa, and Warren would be able to go home again.

Jennifer couldn't wait to get home to start her journal … not one of those "daily entry" diaries with only enough space given to write, "Went to school today. Came home. Had grilled chicken for dinner."

I'll get myself some kind of blank book with no limits, she thought, and no printed-out dates. I'll enter things I truly want to remember and things I should remember, and I'll date the entries myself. I'll call it my "now-and-then journal," so I won't feel guilty if I miss sometimes. But even when nothing exciting is going on, writing my special thoughts actually will help me know what I think, and who I am! That's something of what Nitty Gritty and the Memory Rooms have taught me.

Morgan, they discovered, woke up while they were gone and he was waiting for them with Nakeesha. The party the Chrystelleans had promised them, was being set up for the following day. After that, they could head for home as soon as they wished.

They could see for themselves, then, that Morgan was as good as new. Warren, Willa, and Atta Girl were all there (and Beau, of course, with Atta), and Nitty Gritty reported that the rebuilt Chrystal Gate was almost finished. She'd said they would be able to return to Earth right after the party.

Chapter 31

Party Time

The next morning, Jenny put on the gorgeous party gown that Nitty had given her. In a deep pocket of its very full skirt were two silver "walnuts," one containing her Earth clothes, and the other one holding the Chrystellean disguise she'd been wearing while she was on the surface. This gown and those clothes might come in handy for a costume party or a masquerade, she thought. Willa and Warren were wearing grand finery too, and Warren topped off his glittering suit with Rell's wondrous fruit-bearing hat. He'd swapped it with Rell in return for his Dr. Seuss hat. They were all every bit as gorgeously dressed as she was. What a party this was going to be!

She climbed the stairsteps to Nitty's cave home without hesitation. She nearly danced through the permeable wall that led into the glass cupboard and on into Nitty's cave. Nitty wasn't there, nor Behrrn, Ildirmyrth, Grehssekker, or even Rell. But Nakeesha was waiting to take her to the party. Jenny chattered excitedly, and Nakeesha, smiling, *almost* chattered back. They went across the clearing where the rocking chairs were parked for possible later use.

There was no sign of a party there, so Jennifer followed Nakeesha through the clearing and into the woods. It was the first chance she'd had to walk through the Chrystellean Woods now that color had come to them. She almost forgot about the party as she took in the marvels of the woods, and she did forget about it for a moment when she saw a small, about ten inches tall, teenage girl apparently swimming through the air toward them and a boy about the same size zipping down to them, both flaring with iridescent air bubbles as if they were underwater.

"Who are they, Nakeesha," she asked in a whisper, not wanting to offend the tiny individuals. "I never saw anyone like them when I was in the woods before."

"They're Small Ones," the Prime Minister answered. "They were afraid to come out before this. They live in their own underground places and palaces. But now that Tehrran Tuhlla hasn't been seen or heard from since he was pulled into the mountain's passages, they feel free to come above. There are still a few Ghanglers, his meanest thugs who still try to bully everybody, especially other Ghanglers. These thugs got themselves back into white robes and colored their hair white again, but the other Ghanglers have been having too much fun with brightly colored clothing to pay attention to them."

"That's totally fabulous!" Jennifer exclaimed. She'd thought she had been as happy as she could get, but she felt her heart float a little higher with the joy of it. She hoped this peaceful time would continue for Chrystellea, always!

The tiny girl lighted on Jenny's shoulder and kissed her cheek, with a barely heard, "Thank you, Color Bringer."

The boy hovered in front of her and bowed deeply from the waist, echoing the girl's thanks. Then they both laughed gaily and let themselves drift upward toward that world's suns. Jenny and Nakeesha walked on, and soon those Small Ones and some of their friends were moving with them toward a greater group—the party!

One tiny newcomer was riding a very small, horselike animal that glimmered like mother of pearl. Another was scooting through the air on—a skateboard!

Jenny had been in that forest before when she, Willa, and Atta Girl were dumped on the planet by the white hole in space. But it was as if she had never seen it before. The fallen leaves and other foliage softened the surface underfoot with colors so random that it seemed the trees couldn't quite decide whether the season was spring, summer, or fall. Some trees even seemed to feel that it was winter already, and their dark, bare branches added structure to the beauty of the scene.

The light breeze, though, was definitely spring.

One thing that Jenny couldn't come near to understanding was what lay under the fallen vegetation. Underneath the leaves and flowers shone a clear, shining surface. If it *was* a surface. It seemed to have no substance of its own, even though people and animals of all sizes, and even Jenny herself, were comfortably supported by it.

Jenny, too curious to leave it alone, bent down to touch it. She reached through the leaves and—there was nothing there. Her hand went through it as if it were only air. As she straightened again, she saw that Willa was nearby, just standing up too, after the same kind of exploration. They grinned as they looked at each other, shrugged, joined elbows, and went on. Some things don't have to be understood to be enjoyed.

Music, at first almost too faint to be noticed, was gaining in volume. Of course there was almost always music on that world, except for the Ghangler capitol city, Mimeopolis. Music was a beautiful necessity on the White World, because that's what powered that world's work, except again for the Ghanglers, who had always moved and ruled by the power of the whirlwind. That seemed to be changing now.

This music was different from what they'd heard in the towns and cities. There the music was almost chuckling, as if whatever was going on was delightful and fun. Here in the forest, however, it sounded symphonic; although even by listening carefully, Jennifer couldn't tell what any of the instruments might be.

Now and then, light would fan upward through the fallen leaves, instead of downward through clouds, as on Earth. Jennifer thought it might be a lot like heaven.

She was startled out of her musing when one of the Small People, a princely fellow, hovered directly in front of her, holding out his hands as if asking her to dance. Smiling, she held out hers, and he touched the index finger of each of her hands and began to move in a dance, as the music changed from a symphony to a dance band. *What a world*, she thought again, as she had *so* many times while she was here, and she found herself moving with her partner as if being led by an accomplished, full-sized dancer. Willa had a partner too—a good-looking, full-sized boy and Warren looked embarrassed but pleased as a pretty girl in a flowing gown chose him to dance with.

The music they danced to was lovely and graceful, like ballroom dancing music, and their partners changed so often it made them happily dizzy. The music got faster and livelier, until they could see a perfectly round bandstand floating about four feet above the ground ahead of them. They were playing something lively, a lot like … *rock?* Wow, what a party!

The Small People rocked out with the best of them, and regular-sized people had joined the dance too. Before she knew it, she was dancing with Behrrn! Willa and Morgan were rocking too, and the Newfangler herself was Warren's partner. Jenny had lost track of Rell, but then she located him by the Dr. Seuss hat he'd traded with Warren. He was dancing with a pretty young girl, who was dressed in what must have been her party best. She was leading him through the lively dance moves with a dimpled smile.

When Jenny and the others were thoroughly exhausted, the music slowed and faded and seemed about ready to stop. Then the band broke into a joyous fanfare, and Jenny, Willa, and Atta Girl found themselves alone on a rise in the ground, in the very center of the enormous crowd. Even Beauregard was lost somewhere in the crowd, and Atta Girl was anxiously looking around for him.

The three were surrounded by cheering crowds of White Worlders of all sizes and descriptions, even some of the newly colorful Ghanglers! Instead of their usual white robes, they wore long, colorful ones. Some wore bright, cheery hats too, and some of their robes even had patterns and ruffles! They could hardly be recognized except by their whirlwinds and their height. To Jenny's amazement, they were cheering along with everyone else.

When the fanfare and cheering finally stopped, the crowd neatly parted to open a long, straight pathway, about six feet wide. At the far end, a huge, glittering golden roll of something began to move, slowly at first, then more quickly until they could see, by the red-and-white-striped hat, that it was Rell who was unrolling the shimmering pathway toward the three who were on the mound. The path, or golden carpet, ended right at the feet of the three on the rise, and Rell quickly pulled himself to attention on the side, next to Warren, who was still in the crowd. He was holding what appeared to be … *a digital camera?* He saw her looking, and grinned, using his free hand to pat one of his big pockets, then he started taking pictures again.

Behrrn was coming up the carpet toward them, carrying something draped over his arm. As he approached, Jenny could see that he held three beautifully embroidered sashes, with the title "Dreamsaver" worked into the intricate patterns of their backgrounds.

Behrrn draped the two larger ones over the shoulders of Willa and Jennifer, then he placed the much smaller one over Atta Girl's neck. He gave a short speech, telling everyone in the crowd about how they had helped save the "color memory," which had been fading out of their lives when the earthlings had first come to their planet. At that time, a memory of color was all the people of the White World had, and it was fading. The Dreamsavers had saved it for them and with it the economy of Chrystellea. The three on the hillock felt ever so grand, and the applause was loud and enthusiastic.

But when the small group had barely had time to say a quick thank you, Nitty the Newfangler and Morgan the Magnificent, Wandering Wohtt were coming toward them on the dazzling carpet. Quietly, Behrrn joined those on the hillock and moved Jenny toward the front with Morgan as Nitty came forward with two gloriously embroidered sashes. These were each emblazoned with the words "Color Bringer." The Newfangler motioned Morgan to a spot directly next to Jennifer and carefully draped one of her sashes over Jennifer's shoulder and the other one over Morgan's shoulder. Morgan blushed as Nitty awarded him his, the pastel tips of his fluff turning all rosy pink. "I didn't do anything," he muttered again, but Nitty simply smiled and placed the tips of two dainty fingers on his lips. The applause rang out once again.

Jenny, Willa, and Atta Girl started to go down to join the crowd below, thinking that the ceremony *must* be over. But almost before they had made a move, Behrrn motioned them back. He went down off the hillock and into the crowd. All the while, of course, Warren was busy with his camera, taking pictures and moving from one place to another, as every member of the rescue party who wasn't already on the hillock, joined those already there—even Beauregard, who moved quickly to Atta Girl's side.

Lehna interrupted Warren's picture taking to usher him up on the hillock too. With a few quiet words and gestures, Jenny's brother handed his camera to Rell, showed him how to use it, and took his place next to Jenny.

Ildirmyrth moved onto the far end of the carpet and approached the group, carrying a stack of shining wood plaques with gold plates on the front, each inscribed with a name of one of the rescue party along with the bold and beautiful words "SAVER of our CHILDREN" etched in the gold. He ceremoniously awarded the first three to Jennifer, Willa, and Atta Girl, and then he stepped aside as another masterworker took his place to award the next three, and so on until all of the party had received their awards. Atta Girl and Beauregard received exquisite, tiny versions of those, as well.

When the last award was given the roar of the applause was deafening and went on an on until Behrrn stepped forward and raised his hands. The crowd quickly quieted.

"It's time," he announced in his soft voice that somehow carried to the back rows of the crowd. "It's time for the feasting."

Chapter 32

◆

The Chrystal Gate

Much, much later, the much-awarded and greatly appreciated group, along with all the official award presenters, arrived back at the dream castle. They were urged to rest a bit in a cozy parlor on the ground level of the castle while Behrrn and Nitty went on to put finishing touches on the Chrystal Gate.

While the group relaxed in the parlor's soft easy chairs, the excited conversation continued. They were delightfully stuffed with food from the feast and were totally, happily tired from dancing. Jennifer, Willa, and Warren had changed back into their Earth clothes, but they'd been given the walnut shells containing their elegant party clothes and their regular White World clothes.

They all chatted about everything that had happened until Nitty and Behrrn returned. Jenny, Willa, and Warren were excited to be going home, even though they were sad to be leaving their White World friends again. This time, though, they'd be returning to Earth with Warren's digital camera full of pictures, which hopefully would take the worried looks on their moms' and dads' faces and replace them with looks of dumbfounded amazement. Warren patted the pocket with the camera to reassure them all that it was still there.

After they'd about run out of talk, Nitty and Behrrn returned to lead them to the Chrystal Gate Room, which was itself a wonder.

Behrrn and Nitty had chosen to create the room deeply below the Dreamcastle, to safeguard it from future threats. They assured the group from Earth that it had been dreamed into the dream castle in such a way that no one but Nitty, Behrrn, or Morgan could possibly find it or even redream it.

"How does the gate work?" Willa asked.

"Verily, I doth not know," Nitty Gritty replied. "I know only that it doth work."

"*How* do you know, Nitty?"

"Truly, Jennifer dear, friend Morgan and I have personally tested it. It's right on!"

It was hard to stand in that room and believe that the so-called gate in its center would actually take them home. It looked eerily mysterious in the dusky room, with what seemed to be planets, stars, and even galaxies floating through it on both sides. They could see through that portal to the other side of the room. If they stepped through it, surely that's where it would take them. How could those two chrystal rocks possibly take them clear across universes, to the lilac tree in Jenny's backyard?

But then how had rocking chairs managed to fly? And how had the Chystals brought them here in the first place?

Jennifer stepped forward, the others gathering beside her. But Atta Girl held back as she sadly "spoke" directly to Jenny's heart.

I sssshalll not be goinnng, dearr Jenny, she said. *I ssshall be ssstaying here with Beauregard, wherrre I cannn commmunnnicate with others. The Chrystelleans hhhave offffered ussss a home here in Chryssstellea. I ssshall miss you dreadfully, Jennifer, but I shallll ssstay here with my Beau.*

Even through her shock, Jenny wondered how Atta had learned to communicate so well. She guessed it was all the practice she got this time, here in the White World. She held her arms out toward her cat, and Atta leaped into them. She nestled against Jenny lovingly as Jenny petted her one last time.

"I'll miss you so," Jenny said. "I'll be lonely." As she gently put Atta down she told the small lion. "Take care of her, Beau." He leaned reassuringly against her legs. There was a sympathetic silence for a moment as she turned back toward the gate, and then another voice stopped her in her tracks.

"Hold on there, Missy! 'Tis Marvin here and there be no call for ye to be lonely there on Earth. With yer permission, *I'll* be comin' with ye now. I kin talk *ennywhere*."

Jenny turned back and located the parrot ruffling his feathers anxiously from where he was perched on Rell's shoulder at the back of the group. He had smuggled himself into the Chrystal Room. "That would be marvelous, Marvin," she said after a moment, while still sending her love to Atta's mind and heart. "But there would be dangers for you there and some rules to follow to keep you safe."

"'Tis no matter to me, Miss Jenny. All I needs be some seed and mebbe a cracker or two. And I be longing to read with ye agin and learn how all them stories end."

Jenny looked at him, and his wildly colorful feathers ruffled anxiously as he perched on Rell's shoulder. A grin shone through her tears.

"I'd love to have you, Marvin," she said. "Maybe you can help me write my journal. And maybe I'll even help you write yours."

He quickly fluttered over the onlookers to her shoulder, and she, with Marvin aboard and hand in hand with Willa and Warren, walked through the Chrystal Gate.